BOOK OF SCREAMS

JEFF SZPIRGLAS

illustrated by
STEVEN P. HUGHES

ORCA BOOK PUBLISHERS

For Danielle, Ruby and Léo—and that vial of
mysterious liquid that all my ideas come from —J.S.

Published in Canada and the United States in 2023 by Orca Book Publishers.
orcabook.com

Library and Archives Canada Cataloguing in Publication
Title: Book of screams / Jeff Szpirglas ; illustrated by Steven P. Hughes.
Names: Szpirglas, Jeff, author. | Hughes, Steven P., 1989- illustrator.
Description: Short stories.
Identifiers: Canadiana (print) 20220472858 | Canadiana (ebook) 20220472874 |
ISBN 9781459834095 (softcover) | ISBN 9781459834101 (PDF) | ISBN 9781459834118 (EPUB)
Classification: LCC PS8637.Z65 B66 2023 | DDC jC813/.6—dc23

Library of Congress Control Number: 2022950240

Summary: A delightfully creepy collection of tales about everything from a Jekyll/Hyde homeroom
teacher to a boiler-room ghoul to a kid's wobbly "baby eye," woven between excerpts from a central
story about a girl whose favorite horror author is stealing children's nightmares for his books.

Orca Book Publishers is committed to reducing the consumption of nonrenewable resources in the
production of our books. We make every effort to use materials that support a sustainable future.

Orca Book Publishers gratefully acknowledges the support for its publishing programs provided
by the following agencies: the Government of Canada, the Canada Council for the Arts and the
Province of British Columbia through the BC Arts Council and the Book Publishing Tax Credit.

Cover and interior artwork by Steven P. Hughes.
Edited by Sarah Howden
Design by Troy Cunningham
Old lined paper © Babybird-Stock

Printed and bound in Canada.

26   25   24   23   •   1   2   3   4

region of waterloo
ARTS FUND

Jeff Szpirglas gratefully acknowledges the financial
support of the Region of Waterloo Arts Fund.

CONTENTS:

MASKS 1

i. TANYA AND THE INK 7

THE WORDS ON THE WALL 16

BABY EYES 29

ii. TANYA AND THE INK 38

THE TAR 42

DUST TO DUST 61

iii. TANYA AND THE INK 75

SUPPLY AND DEMAND 87

A TIGHT FIT 102

iv. TANYA AND THE INK 117

STREAMED 126

THE FEEDER 137

v. TANYA AND THE INK 161

MASKS

You have to wear a mask when you go to school now. That's the rule.

You have to wear a mask when you go to the store. Or if you get too close to somebody. That's the rule too. You don't want to spread the germs.

I don't mind. Some kids do.

I wear a mask whenever I need to.

Do you know what, though? Sometimes I take the mask off. Sometimes I just want to feel the air on my face, so when nobody's looking, I take a break.

Did you know I wore a mask before everyone else had to? I wore the mask so much that I didn't really have any friends. At least, not until everybody else started wearing masks. That leveled the playing field.

And then I became friends with Rayaan.

Rayaan asked me to come over to his house. Nobody had asked me to come over to their house in a long, long time.

But we couldn't go into Rayaan's house. He wasn't allowed to have friends inside, even with the masks on. The germs, remember?

That was okay, because we could play in his backyard. As long as we kept our masks on.

So we started off in Rayaan's backyard, but it was pretty small. It was hard to play a good game of anything back there, so I got an idea. I decided to take him to my backyard instead.

We walked down the street. I took him to where I live, at the end of the road.

Rayaan stopped when we reached my place.

He looked at the fence, and then he looked past it. "Where are we going?"

"Come on, you'll see," I told him.

Rayaan shook his head.

"Oh, don't be a baby. This is gonna be fun!"

I could tell Rayaan was thinking it over. I needed to be really convincing. "We'll stay outside," I told him. "I know about the rules."

"You're sure about this?" he said.

"Trust me. There's lots of room to run around."

Finally Rayaan agreed.

I pulled open the gate, and we went in.

We ran around for a long time. There's a lot of space in my yard. We played catch and keep away and tag, and we ran ourselves ragged. Rayaan even seemed to forget those nervous feelings he was having, which was good. He got really into our game of tag, right up until he tripped over one of the big stones in the yard. He fell to the ground with a heavy thud. Then I heard him start to gasp for air.

I moved closer to him. "Rayaan, you okay?"

I must have been too close, because he held up his hand. "You've got to keep your distance!" he told me. Or that's what he was trying to tell me, but he was so busy gasping for air that the words just wheezed out of him, like he was an accordion somebody had stepped on.

I could see him fumbling around for something in the muddy ground nearby. But he was wheezing so hard he couldn't even reach it. Instead he clawed at his mask, pulling the whole thing off.

I saw what he was looking for. It was his puffer. I bent down and grabbed it for him.

Rayaan reached out to me, and I let him have the puffer. I watched as he jammed one end into his mouth and depressed the button. There was a little hiss of air, and Rayaan took in a deep breath. Then another and another. I watched and waited until the wheezing had died down and Rayaan had taken his inhaler out of his mouth. He was just sitting there, slowly breathing the air in and out of his lungs. His chest moved up and down.

We didn't say anything for a bit. I listened to the wind rustle through the branches of the trees. At the end of the road, we were far enough away from the rumble of cars and trucks that there was some real peace and quiet.

Rayaan looked at me. "Why did you take me here?"

I blinked. "To play."

"But *here*?"

"You took your mask off," I said, pointing at him. He'd broken the rule. I mean, he'd had to. He'd needed his puffer. But it had given me an idea.

"I had an asthma attack," he said.

"It's okay. I'm pretty sure we're keeping a safe distance," I told him. "I can take my mask off too."

"But why did we come *here*?" I was too busy reaching up to take off the cloth mask around my mouth and nose to answer him at first. That was okay. He pretty much answered his own question when he added, "We're in a graveyard."

Then I reached around behind my head again. I really needed to breathe as deeply as Rayaan. I knew how good it felt when you had the air right on your face. "Here, let me just take this mask off."

"You took your mask off," Rayaan said, pointing to the piece of fabric balled up in my hand.

"No, silly," I told him. "The *other* one."

He looked like he was going to say something, but he stopped when he saw what I was doing. I dug my fingers into the flesh behind my neck. I dug them in real deep. I made a little hole there and pulled the skin open.

Rayaan screamed.

I pulled harder, and the mask slowly peeled off my head in one piece. The air hit my face then, and I took in a deep breath. Oh, it felt so good to have the wind and the coolness on my face again!

Rayaan saw the real me, and he didn't stop screaming. He screamed louder. He screamed so hard that he started wheezing again.

I gently placed the mask on top of the stone standing closest to us. "Look," I told him, pointing to the stone. I pointed at the letters etched into the smooth surface. "This is my home. I can come and go anytime I want."

Rayaan was trying to get up. Trying to run away. But he couldn't stand and use the puffer at the same time, so he just collapsed back to the soft, muddy earth.

"Don't worry," I said. I knew how to fix his problem. All that screaming and not enough air. I stepped toward him. "You'll feel better when I take *your* mask off too."

Then I reached out to show him how it was done.

For Tanya,
Stay Scared!
Joel Southland

part one

"So where do you get your ideas?"

Tanya couldn't believe he was actually here. She knew that Joel Southland toured schools all across the country. She just couldn't believe he'd actually attended hers—and just in time for Halloween too!

She had all of his books. Tanya was not an avid reader, but she liked scary stories. She remembered the first book of Joel's that she'd encountered. It was at the school book fair, which came around three times a year.

Usually Tanya would buy some sticker book tied to her favorite TV show and think little else about it. But then she'd noticed Joel Southland's *Stories to Melt Your Mind* on account of its terrifying cover illustration, which depicted a boy having his head set on fire by a pair of disembodied hands. The boy had this agonizing look on his face, and the idea of a skeleton setting a head on fire? It gave Tanya instant chills. So she'd demanded that her parents buy it.

It had turned out to be just the kind of book Tanya was after. Although it was novel-length, it was a series of stories, meaning that if one of them sucked, she could just move on to the next one.

She'd been awake the last several nights, not because of any of Southland's stories (although she had reread a bunch of them in the last few weeks), but because she was trying to figure out what to ask him.

"So where *do* you get your ideas?" Ms. Monroe asked again.

Tanya rolled her eyes, although she didn't let anyone see it.

She and her class were assembled in the library's open space reserved for presentations and class activities. Most of her classmates had been talking and fidgeting, which was the norm with presentations, but it hadn't taken long for Joel Southland to capture their attention. He'd begun with a slideshow of all kinds of nightmarish imagery, big pictures of spiders and snakes and ghouls, and then he'd started a conversation about the kinds of things that scared the kids.

"Author talks," one of her classmates had joked, but Southland had just rolled with the hecklers. He'd probably seen a lot of them in his time, and soon enough he'd managed to get even their attention and had all the kids writing their own scary stories on the spot.

"Anyhow, you're not wrong," Southland said, eyeing the crowd. "I do get lots of ideas from these school visits. From talking to you about all the things you fear. I like to work your fears into my stories. It's what makes them more real." He stopped and surveyed the room, and Tanya flinched visibly when their eyes met. Not because he was creepy or anything. No, Joel Southland seemed friendly, in a Dad type of way. It was just weird being in the same room with her idol.

The presentation ended with a number of students sharing the writing they'd composed during the session. Tanya raised her hand to share, but there were, like, sixty kids in the library, and her hand was buried among the thirty or so others that went up in the air in front of her. Similarly, when it was time to wish him goodbye, the author found himself mobbed by students who all wanted autographs. Most of them hadn't brought books along, but that was okay, because Southland had come armed with a stack of signed bookmarks. He made sure to hand them out to each and every one who asked.

All the while, Tanya stood at the back of the library. The recess bell had rung, and her peers were starting to leave in droves. The ones who hung back were the ones who found time with a real, famous author more appealing than horsing around on the blacktop outside.

Tanya waited some more, until she was the last one left. She took a deep breath and then bravely stepped toward him.

She drew nearer, but he was busy powering down his laptop computer and putting his sample books away, and it was only when she said, in a fairly meek voice, "Mr. Southland?" that he looked in her direction.

"Hello?"

Tanya stood there, unsure what to say.

"You were at the presentation," he said, looking at her. "In the back."

She blinked. "You saw me?"

"I'm sorry I didn't get a chance to hear your story."

Tanya looked down at the paper in her hands. She'd rolled it up like a scroll, but she was so nervous that she'd crumpled it in her fist.

"I can still read it, though, can't I?"

Tanya nodded. She unclenched her fist and held the paper toward him.

He took it from her, eyes scanning the page. "It's Tanya, right?"

"How did you know—?"

"You put your name on the page."

"Oh." Tanya smiled, blushing. She hated blushing, especially in front of *world-famous authors*.

The recess bell rang, which meant she had to leave to get back to class, but it also helped to end the awkward conversation.

Then Southland reached into his jacket pocket and pulled out a bookmark. He signed it and handed it to her. "Here. For you."

Tanya looked down at the inscription.

FOR TANYA,
STAY SCARED!

And then, from behind, she heard Ms. Monroe's voice. "Come on, Tanya. Leave Mr. Southland to finish up. And you need to get back to class."

"Thanks," she said. "Keep writing those great stories."

She backed away, bumping into a stack of books and knocking them over.

"You okay?" Southland asked.

"Oh yeah," said Tanya, still blushing. "Thanks!"

Obviously, Tanya was going to read some Joel Southland stories before falling asleep. She ignored the late hour indicated by the clock on her nightstand and continued to read horrifying tale after horrifying tale, until she was sure that even her parents had nodded off and gone to bed.

Tanya knew it was time to turn out the lights when she noticed she was blinking so much and for so long that she'd begun to lose track of the words on the page.

She reached for something to keep her place and remembered the signed bookmark from one Joel A. Southland on her nightstand. She picked it up and studied the message, scrawled in black ink.

FOR TANYA, STAY SCARED!

More like, have a good sleep, Tanya thought sarcastically.

She was just beginning to put the bookmark into the pages, just beginning to close the book, when she saw something out of the corner of her eye.

Tanya dismissed it as a case of the sleepies, because what she thought she saw was the signature on the bookmark *move*.

Tanya shook herself back into alertness, opened the book and looked closely at the bookmark. She held it under the lamp by her nightstand.

The squiggle was still there.

FOR TANYA, STAY SCARED!

Just like it had been, only...

Only it had changed.

Tanya was certain of it suddenly, and the certainty sent a surge of adrenaline coursing through her. She blinked, but now her heart was thudding in her chest, and her eyes were wide.

The letters of the signature were all still there, but they were not the same. The *T* in her name, for instance, was shaped differently. And so were the two s's in *Stay scared!*

Well, now Tanya *was* scared.

She flipped the bookmark over just to be sure that it wasn't double-sided, that she hadn't missed some silly clue, and when she flipped it back over again, she gasped.

The letters had changed completely this time.

Yessssssssss, they said, like they knew she was watching.

Then the letters ran together, as if the ink had suddenly gone all wet, and pooled into one big black squiggle. Tanya let go of the bookmark, and it slipped down the narrow gap between her bed and the nightstand.

She lay there for a moment, heart thumping, not daring to move.

After a moment or two of quiet, she peered over the edge of the bed. Tanya could see the bookmark on the floor. All she could see was the blank back side. It lay there, unmoving, and Tanya just stared at it for a long moment. Maybe a minute, maybe more.

This was ridiculous, she finally decided. She was in one of those weird states when her imagination was running away with her. Ink didn't suddenly get wet and reassemble into other letters, and if she reached down and pulled the bookmark back up, she'd see that it would just tell her to *Stay scared!*

And that's what she did. She reached down—so far that she had to wedge her shoulder between the bed and the nightstand, and even then her fingers just barely brushed against the wooden floorboards, so it took a few tries before she managed to lift the bookmark off the floor with her fingertips. She let out a sigh of relief as she pulled the bookmark back up toward her, then flipped it over.

The ink was still wet, and now it was coiled like a snake. Tanya could swear that some of the black wasn't just ink but a shadow, because the ink had *lifted* itself off the bookmark, and before Tanya could scream, it leapt up at her.

She dropped the bookmark and leapt back on the bed, but the ink was too fast. It landed on the back of her hand with a cold splat. Tanya tried to swat it off but succeeded only in smudging the ink.

Now it was smeared across the back of her hand *and* under her opposite fingers. It bit into her skin like a jet of ice water, so cold that it made the blood in her veins freeze. She could feel it on her the way you can feel it when a bug is on your skin and madly scuttling across your arm.

The ink thinned out into a liquid black ribbon, stretching the splotch on the back of her hand across her arm and around to the other side, where it blended in with the bluish veins on her wrists. The residual smear on her opposite fingertip had changed from a large smudge into a smaller dot of ink, but it too was traveling across her hand and up her arm. It disappeared in her sleeve. She batted at her arms, but Tanya could feel the ink under her pajamas tightening its grip. Her pulse pounded like someone had shoved blood-pressure cuffs around her upper arms. She began to breathe in quick spurts, trying to

cry out, but the sound had been strangled out of her. She felt the two ribbons of ink work farther up her arms, toward her shoulders, then to her neck.

"No," she gasped.

The ink pulsed and throbbed in sync with her own frantic heartbeats.

She ran to the bathroom, to the mirror, digging her hands into the cool porcelain of the sink and watching, horrified, as the two little snakes of ink worked their way up the sides of her neck. She tried to pull the ink off, but it just smudged again, then changed back into the inky ribbon, now at her chin, running across her face, right to her open eyes.

"No!"

She squeezed them shut, but she could feel the ice-cold ink probing her closed eyelids, trying to seek a way inside, and then Tanya felt the ink pushing at the corners of her eyes, getting under the lids, getting *behind* her eyes, and she opened her mouth to scream—

THE WORDS ON THE WALL

"What did you want us to do again?"

"You're gathering samples of texture," said Ms. Tobin.

"Samples of…"

"Texture, texture. How something *feels*."

Anton shifted his weight from foot to foot, holding the paper and the crayon in his hands. He'd come to this country with limited understanding of the English language and was still learning its nuances.

Ms. Tobin took Anton's hand, the one with the paper in it, and put it against the yellow cinder-block wall. Maybe the hallways had been painted a more pleasing shade of cream back in the day, but the passing of time and the constant commotion of hundreds of children passing through the hallways, running their fingers along the bumpy surfaces, had stained it the shade of yellow that was bordering on *gross*.

"You'll need to color," she said, plucking the blue crayon from Anton's hand and rubbing it against the paper on the wall. The rough pattern from the cinder blocks came through on the paper.

Anton smiled. "Good job, Ms. Tobin!"

Ms. Tobin exhaled deeply. She handed the paper and the crayon back to Anton. "Find other textures," she said.

"Other textures." Anton nodded. "Like the other wall?"

Ms. Tobin shrugged. "Suré. The other wall. Or why not the vent over there? Other things in the hallway. We are gathering samples of texture for art class."

"Textures," Anton said, feeling the word roll around on his tongue. Anton noticed his tongue. It too had a texture.

He gave Ms. Tobin a nod of affirmation.

"Be back in ten minutes," she said, pointing to the clock on the wall.

"Ten minutes, yes," Anton said. He looked at his peers moving down the hallway, paper and crayons in hand, busily rubbing.

Anton nodded. Finding textures. It wasn't a challenging activity, beyond his needing a minute to understand what Ms. Tobin was actually talking about. It was easy, really, and he was out here in the hallway, out of class, coloring with crayons. What more could he ask for?

Anton turned his paper over so that the clean side was showing. He put it up against a bare patch of wall and rubbed the crayon back and forth, back and forth.

As he did so, letters appeared on the paper.

English letters.

Anton stopped. He narrowed his eyes, lifting the paper

away from the wall and staring at it quizzically. He ran his fingers along the painted surface. He didn't feel any change in the texture to signify where the letters were coming from. He tilted his head to stare at it from a different angle, hoping to reveal the source of the letters, but no.

"Hmm," Anton said.

This was interesting.

He placed the paper back against the wall and rubbed with his crayon. He watched the letters, all uppercase, form.

H-E.

"He," Anton said. Maybe it was the beginning of a sentence? He kept rubbing. More letters appeared.

H-E-L-P.

"Help," Anton said. He didn't know many English words yet, but he knew that one. And the word that followed. "Help me," he said, and now he felt a shiver run through him.

He lifted the paper off the wall, staring at the rough surface of the cinder block one more time, hoping the words would make themselves seen.

Then he looked back at the letters on the paper. *HELP ME*. They were written in a child's messy scrawl. Anton looked over his shoulder at a boy and girl from his class walking down the hallway toward him. "Jason," he said to the boy, waving his paper excitedly. "Look what I found!"

Jason stepped up to Anton and grabbed the paper. "*Help me?*"

Anton pointed to the wall. "On the wall," he said. "The words are on the wall!"

Jason looked to where Anton was pointing and shook his head. "There's nothing there, Anton."

"Yes! See?" And Anton grabbed the paper back, found a white space on the page, laid it against the wall and began to rub madly with his crayon. "It's here. I found it right here!"

All he got was a page full of blue.

Anton didn't understand. He shook his head.

"Whatever, Anton," Jason said. The girl had already gone back to class, and now Jason followed.

Ms. Tobin's head popped out of the doorway, and she found Anton standing there, looking dumbfounded. "Five minutes, Anton," she said, pointing to the clock.

Just because no one else believed him didn't mean Anton wasn't right. Later that day, at recess, after everybody else had stampeded outside to the playground, Anton paced down the hallway. He was ready to head out if asked to, so he was dressed in his winter jacket (ugh, the winter in this country was the worst!), his hat, his boots. But he had taken several pieces of paper from the blue recycling bin, and he had a crayon. He moved down the hallway until he reached the spot where he'd found the first message.

He rubbed the paper against the wall. This time it was a red crayon, and all he got was red on the paper.

Red, red, red! No words, no—

Wait.

There was something there, at the edge of the page. Not a word, not even a letter yet. It was just the curve of something, half off the page. Anton dropped the paper, letting it flutter to the floor, and dug out the next blank piece. He placed it right beside the spot where he'd found the curve, and now, as he rubbed, he saw another word appear.

COLD.

Anton nodded. "Outside? It is cold. It is winter," he said aloud. He lifted the page off the wall and turned it over so he had another blank side to work with.

"Are you cold?" he asked the space on the wall where the word had been.

This was stupid. The wall would not talk back to him.

If anything, he was just going to find the word *COLD* on the wall a second time.

Heck, the words *HELP ME* were probably still there somewhere, and Anton had just been unable to find them again. It was some kid's idea of a prank—maybe even Jason's. He was going to make a fool of Anton, and this was part of his plan.

Nevertheless, Anton already had the page out. Already had the crayon in his hand. "You're cold, right?" he said to the wall, laughing at his own foolishness, then moving the crayon over the paper, waiting for the word *COLD* to form on the page, only…

"No," Anton said.

He was saying this to himself, but also saying the word that was on the wall.

NO, the wall said. Anton had only filled out part of the page in the red crayon, and now he scribbled over the rest of the paper so that he could see the full message appear, in the same scratchy scrawl.

NOT COLD. COLDER.

Anton shook his head. He should stop, he told himself. It wasn't Jason, and it wasn't a prank.

He looked past the wall. *The haunted wall?* Looked down the empty hallway, at the indoor shoes strewn this way and that, the overturned waste bins, the windowed doors at the far end, where he could see the kids outside, still playing. He should leave this place and join them. He should not keep talking to the wall.

"Colder," Anton said, biting his lip. "What is colder?"

He moved a few steps closer to the far doors and found a spot on the wall. A new spot. He made a new rubbing. And new words greeted him.

WARMER.

"But outside is colder," Anton said. "And we are close to outside."

He took more steps toward the doors. Put the next paper down on the wall and rubbed.

YOU ARE GETTING WARMER.

It took Anton a moment to remember that this was an expression. Getting colder. Getting warmer. Ms. Tobin had used those words when playing a game where she wanted the students to find something. And then he recalled the first words the wall had written for him. "Help me," he said again.

He was getting warmer.

"Where are you?" he asked the wall after taking a few more steps toward the exit doors. "Do you want me to help you?"

He took another piece of paper and rubbed it. *HOT.* Anton looked around.

He was standing next to a door.

The door had a sign that read *BOILER ROOM.*

"Yes," Anton said. "The boiler room *is* hot. Is that what you want?"

HELP ME, said the wall. And when Anton asked how, the wall told him: *FIND ME*.

Anton nodded.

He put the paper into his pocket. He put his hand on the doorknob to turn it.

And that's when the bell rang.

The next bell to ring was the one that ended the school day. Anton was old enough to walk home by himself. His parents were both out working at their jobs. They wouldn't be home until much later. He had time to finish this, to solve the mystery.

He tried to get Jason to solve it with him. He showed Jason the papers he'd gathered at recess, explaining as clearly as he could how the words had been changing.

"You want to break into the boiler room," Jason said.

"Yes," Anton said excitedly. "We need to help."

"I like breaking into places," Jason said.

It turned out Jason was good at it too.

He used an old plastic card to jimmy the door open. The boys were greeted with a blast of hot air from the furnace deep within the bowels of the boiler room. Anton slowly closed the door behind him before turning on the lights. He did not want to get caught down here.

"So what now?" Jason asked.

Anton took the paper and rubbed it against the wall closest to him.

Just a splash of red color appeared on the page. Was it only the hallway wall that spoke to Anton? He was here, where the words had told him to come. What now?

"So tell me again why we're breaking into this place," Jason said.

"Not now," Anton snapped, waving him off. The words would come. They *had* to.

"What are you doing here?" a voice boomed from behind them.

Anton jumped. Jason screamed.

The boys turned to see the silhouette of a tall man in the now-open doorway.

"Getting the flip out of here," Jason said, running quickly and sidestepping the imposing frame of the man now entering the boiler room.

"Mr. O'Connor?" Anton said.

He was the school caretaker. He looked like he should be on a wrestling team. Maybe in another life he was.

And although he was an older man, with wispy gray hair that thinned to a bald patch on top, he was still built as strong and sturdy as the walls that had been talking to Anton. "You're not supposed to be in here," Mr. O'Connor said.

"I am trying to help," Anton returned.

"You're going to get yourself into a heap of trouble, is what you're doing."

"No. You don't understand," Anton said. Then he showed Mr. O'Connor the pages. "Somebody needs my help," he said uncertainly.

Mr. O'Connor looked at the words. Looked at the printing. His eyes went big. "Where did you get these?"

Anton motioned to the walls. "They were written for me."

"That's impossible."

"Yes, I know." Anton smiled weakly. Nobody believed him.

"That's Geoff Alcock's handwriting."

Anton shrugged.

"Why would they tell you about Geoff Alcock?" Mr. O'Connor wondered aloud. "Nobody's heard that story in years."

"Who is Geoff Al…" Anton tried to say the last name.

"Alcock," Mr. O'Connor said. "He went to this school, you know. Years ago. When I was a kid."

"Oh," said Anton.

"He didn't make any friends. The other kids teased him. I teased him too," Mr. O'Connor admitted. He stepped farther into the room, letting the door slam behind him and forcing Anton back a few steps. "We didn't know how hard he would take it," he continued after a moment of reflection. His eyes got misty.

"Something happened to him?"

"Story goes, he ran away from some of the kids who taunted him. Got locked in the boiler room overnight. Tried to stay warm."

Mr. O'Connor gave a nod to the metal bulk of the furnace. They were much closer to it now.

"There was a fire. They found what was left of him the next day."

"He…died?"

Mr. O'Connor gave a deep sigh.

Anton understood. There were ghosts in his country too. "He wants my help," said Anton. He looked around the room. "How can we help you?" he asked.

Mr. O'Connor shook his head. "I don't think that's the way this works."

The walls deeper in the room were covered with all kinds of pipes and electrical equipment. There wasn't a clear smooth place to make a rubbing. No place except the surface of the furnace.

Anton put his hand against the metal, on the side away from where the open flame was. It wasn't hot here.

Mr. O'Connor frowned. "You're not going to find anything there."

"Trust me," said Anton.

He began to run the crayon over the paper, and sure enough, now came words.

HELP ME.

"How?" said Anton. "How do we help?" He placed the paper back on the metal.

Mr. O'Connor was shaking his head. "This isn't right."

"What is it? What do you want?" Anton asked.

"He wants to come back," Mr. O'Connor said.

Anton turned to face the custodian. He narrowed his eyes. "How would he do that?"

"It's taken him some time," said Mr. O'Connor. "He's been waiting for just the right fit."

"Just the right fit?" Anton shook his head. Was this another English expression?

"I know his handwriting," Mr. O'Connor said. "Been here a long time. I kept seeing it on the walls. Kept wiping it off. Cleaned the walls a lot. With all different kinds of cleaners. I even painted over them a few times. I thought I was going crazy, you see. Thought it was just me."

"That's what I thought too," said Anton, meeting Mr. O'Connor's eyes.

"I never got over what we did to him," Mr. O'Connor continued. Anton noticed that the caretaker was moving closer to him and the furnace. "So I stayed. Geoff was here too, obviously. Not in body, of course. But here in the school, in the air, on the walls..."

"You're too close," Anton said as Mr. O'Connor moved into Anton's personal space bubble, pushing him back against the flat face of the furnace where there was an opening at waist height.

"You're a good kid," Mr. O'Connor said, sniffing, "but a promise is a promise. And Geoff thinks you're just the right fit."

"Right fit for what?"

Anton felt it before he turned.

Something pushing up from *inside* the furnace, along his back. Something hard and bony pressing out through the opening.

He turned.

The hands and arms were charred black. No skin left on them. Fingers just skeletal claws.

Anton opened his mouth to scream.

Then a head pushed through the opening at the middle of the furnace. The eyes were burned out. The hair singed. Even the teeth were black as soot.

That face. That horrible face!

It even opened its mouth to speak, in a voice as raspy and dry as ashes.

"You are boiling hot," the voice said, and the hands grabbed hold of Anton, pulling him down toward the burned face.

Jason didn't see Anton at school the next day. That didn't seem like a big deal. Maybe he was sick. Kids got sick all the time. But the way he'd left Anton, in the boiler room with Mr. O'Connor coming in? It didn't sit well with Jason.

Anton had been obsessed with the words on the wall.

Jason had never seen any words.

It was just a silly prank. Just something to try to fool him with.

Still…

Jason shook his head. It might have been some kind of prank, but Anton had been so convinced.

Jason didn't want to look like an idiot, rubbing the walls with a crayon like some kid in kindergarten, so he waited until the final bell had rung and everyone had left. He waited until the hallways were as quiet as a dying breath. Then he grabbed a piece of paper and a pencil, found the patch of wall near his classroom that Anton had been so worried about and ran the pencil across the page, back and forth, back and forth.

"Ridiculous," he said to himself under his breath.

But then he ran the pencil across more of the page.

And then he saw the words.

JASON, YOU ARE GETTING WARMER.

BABY EYES

Jules woke up screaming. She clamped a hand to her face.
"Mom, come quick!"

Her eyes were squeezed shut. She heard the heavy thumping
of running footsteps, the swinging of the squeaky hinges, then
felt her mother's hand on her shoulder. It was warm and reas-
suring, but it did not make the pain go away.

"What's wrong?"

"It's my eye," she said, trying to squeeze the pain away.
Her muscles were so tense she thought they might snap like
elastics pulled past their breaking point.

"Let me see," her mom said.

Jules kept her hand pressed against her face.

"Please, Jules. Let me take a look at it." She tried to pull
her daughter's hand away from her face, but Jules held it tightly
in place.

"It's okay," her mom said. "I think I know what's wrong. I just need to see."

Jules took a deep breath. She felt her muscles relax slightly. Enough for her mom to slowly pull her hand away.

"Come on now," her mom said. "Open it up. Let's take a look."

"Something feels wrong."

"Wrong?"

Jules shook her head, not to disagree with her mother but because it was her head that was feeling strange. "My left eye," she said, her voice going quiet, which it always did when she got *really* scared. "It feels...*loose.*"

And then she opened her eyes. Jules saw her mother react. She didn't look worried, but when Jules jerked her head, she could feel the eye move.

Without saying another word, Jules put the palm of her hand back against her eye and, keeping the other open, got up from the bed. She pushed past her mother and closed her bedroom door so she could see her reflection in the full-length mirror hung on it.

After taking a shaky breath, she pulled her hand away and stared.

The eye looked wrong. It should have been fixed firmly in the socket. That's what eyes did. But the flesh around Jules's eyeball was loose. It was like someone had been tugging at her eye socket and stretched it out of shape, like the collar of a sweater. Folds of skin hung limply over her eyeball, which jiggled in its socket with each breath Jules took.

Jules gritted her teeth and inhaled sharply.

"I see," Jules's mom said, reaching out to tenderly run her finger along the loose skin. Jules flinched and turned away, but her mom took hold of her shoulder. Maybe a bit too firmly for her liking. "Don't worry. That's perfectly normal."

"My eye is loose," Jules said, aghast.

"Maybe it will even come out by breakfast," her mom said with a smile.

"*Come out?!*"

"It's just a baby eye. Nothing to worry about." Her mother's tone was calm and measured.

Jules shook her head in disbelief. "What are you talking about!"

"You know, like baby teeth. Those came out, and you were just fine. And just as worried as you are right now."

Jules whipped around to face her mother, and that's when it happened. The force of turning her head so quickly was all that was needed. The eye launched out of the socket, sailed through the air and fell to the wooden floor with an audible *thunk*.

Jules stared at it with her other eye for a good few seconds before she opened her mouth to scream.

As she shrieked, feeling a numbing terror she'd never before experienced, her mom quietly bent down to retrieve the slimy orb between her thumb and index finger. She carefully picked it up and brought it over to Jules's face so she could see it. It was completely devoid of the muscles and tissues that would have kept it fixed in the socket. It was like Jules was staring at a white grape, marred only by the dotted brown disc of her iris. "Let's go put it in a jar so it doesn't get squashed under your pillow," her mom said brightly.

"She put it *where*?"

"Under my pillow. She thinks the eyeball fairy is going to come and take it away."

"Dude, that's disgusting."

Jules couldn't believe her mother had made her go to school after all this. She'd put a pad over the the eye socket and wrapped Jules's head with gauze, then sent her off with a freshly packed lunch and everything. Dan was the first friend Jules encountered in the playground, and she did her best to explain what had been going on since she'd woken up in the middle of the night with her eye throbbing.

Dan paused and thought carefully about everything Jules told him. "Do you get any money for it?" he asked finally.

"Maybe. How much do you think I can get?"

"Probably a lot. It's an eye, right? You've got dozens of teeth, and only two eyes. I'd say at least twenty bucks."

The idea of an eyeball fairy was ridiculous, but then again, so was losing a baby eyeball. It was so ridiculous that Jules didn't tell anyone but Dan about it at school. Even the note she'd brought in from home wasn't the truth. It said Jules had scratched her cornea, that it would heal in a day and to leave the gauze on.

Jules unwrapped the gauze from her head only when she'd returned to the safety of home. All day she had felt something brewing beneath the bandage. It was like an itch, but there was nothing there to scratch.

Her mom would not be home until later, after work, so it was up to Jules alone to inspect what lay beneath. She tossed the gauze into the trash in the downstairs bathroom and pulled the pad away from her eye. She stared into the mirror at the socket. It had been empty that morning, but now Jules could see there was something there, pushing through the mass of flesh. A new eye.

It was still hidden by the tender red muscle that was growing around it, and when Jules tried to look around the room, the new eye just hung lazily in place, and her vision was blurred.

"This is not normal," she told herself. When she used her phone to search online for information about "baby eyes," all Jules got were pictures of babies and websites about the vision of infants. Not helpful.

The doorbell rang.

Jules turned away from the mirror. She waited, and the bell sounded again, echoing through the tiled hallway in the foyer.

Cripes! There was no one else home, and the bandage was gone. She hoped whoever was standing outside would just go away, but the bell kept ringing, like some little kid was playing pranks outside.

Dang it! Jules edged out of the bathroom. She found a pair of sunglasses on the side table and put them on. They were her mom's, way too big and old-fashioned, and Jules was sure they looked ridiculous on her, but the bell wouldn't stop ringing.

Jules unlocked the door and swung it open. "Hey, enough's enou—"

It wasn't a kid.

The figure at the door was unusually tall and wearing a black cloak. A long hood hung over its face.

Before Jules could fully register what she was seeing, the figure stepped forward, placing a booted foot between the door and the frame. Even when Jules used all her might to try to slam the door shut, it bounced harmlessly off the foot as if the boot was made of lead.

The figure thumped inside and moved toward Jules.

"No," she said, staggering back. She slipped and collided butt-first with the floor tiles, knocking the sunglasses off her face.

The figure paused, regarding Jules.

"WHERE IS IT?" The voice slithered out from beneath the hood.

"Please don't hurt me!" Jules cried.

"I MUST HAVE IT!"

"Have what?"

The figure did not respond in words. It simply leaned forward, closer to Jules, and a pair of gloved hands reached up to pull back its hood.

There should have been a whole face there. But the head that was revealed had no discernable nose, or ears, or mouth. Only the eyes stared back at Jules. But there weren't just two. The whole head was covered in eyes, which blinked open and closed and seemed to track everywhere at once.

Jules gasped.

The eyes blinked at different points on the creature's face, snapping open and shut like a cluster of clams exposed to the swell of a shallow tide. "YOUR MOTHER SAID TO EXPECT ME," said the voice. Jules could see it was coming

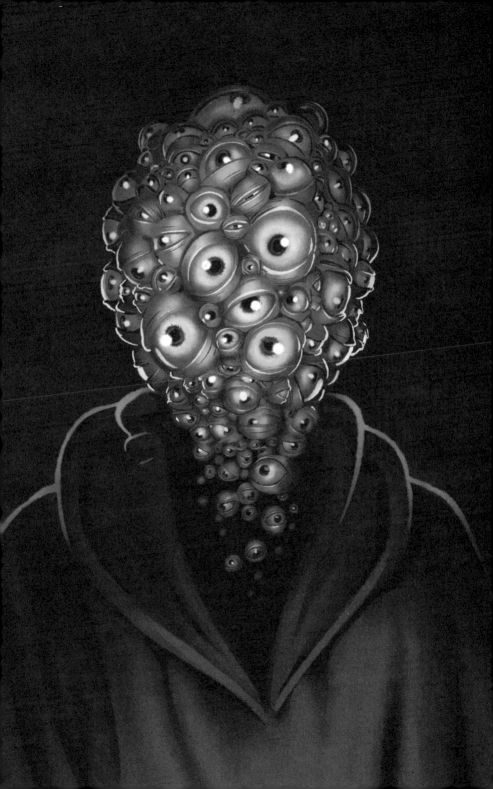

from some of the eyes, which blinked in sync with the creature's words.

"This is not happening," Jules told herself.

Hearing this, the Eye Fairy (at least, that was what her
mom had called it) loomed closer still, so that Jules could
see her terrified reflection looking back from the mosaic of
glistening, staring eyes, which kept moving closer until her
face was all she could see.

Jules woke up screaming.

She clamped a hand to her head. Something felt wrong.
Dead wrong.

What a nightmare!

The door swung open, and in came her mom. Jules sat
up in bed, and that just made it feel worse.

"What's wrong?"

Jules still felt ice-cold stabs of fear pulsing through her.
"Mom, I had the weirdest dream."

"That's been known to happen with what you're going
through."

Jules looked at her mom. "You're not talking about the
eye," she said, her voice choked to a whisper.

"The baby eye, yes."

"That was real?"

Her mother smiled. "And your new eye is growing in *so
well,*" she said, beaming.

Jules felt waves of terror shaking her whole body. Her
hands and arms trembled. She tried to open her mouth to

speak, but the words wouldn't come. Her neck! She could feel little folds in her skin around the base of it as she prodded with her fingertips, and she could feel where it was already coming loose with each movement.

Jules tried to move, but her head wobbled suddenly, tearing at the loose flesh on the side of her neck. She opened her mouth to scream, but her head toppled right off and fell to the floor with a heavy thud before she could make a sound.

Suddenly blinded, Jules leaped out of bed. She clawed at the air. A horrific gurgle came bubbling out of the opening where her neck ended. A pool of thick, sticky liquid was already sealing up the opening.

"Oh, that?" she heard her mother say. "Don't worry about that. It's just your baby *head*!"

part two

Tanya put down the book.

It took her a moment to realize how heavily she was breathing. There was something about the story that was pulling at her thoughts, peeling them back like Band-Aids not quite ready to reveal the wounds underneath. She winced.

It was déjà vu, like she'd experienced it before, like something she'd dreamed...

Tanya flipped back to the cover and stared at it. Joel Southland's *Book of Screams*. She shook the thought from her head.

Her mother had bought it for her, excited to have found it displayed at the bookstore. "How does he manage to write so quickly?" Tanya's mother had wondered aloud. "It's like he puts out a new book every couple of months. He must be making a fortune."

Tanya went back and thumbed through the story, rereading it word for word. She read it again and then closed the book.

None of the other stories contained within its pages felt like such a stab in the guts.

Tanya closed her eyes and took a deep breath. It wasn't that Southland's writing was so remarkable that it filled her head with horrific visions—this was different. None of the other stories had produced quite the same effect as this last one.

It was as vivid as some kind of waking dream, and when Tanya opened her eyes, she remembered.

The story wasn't just a story.

It *was* her dream.

Instinctively Tanya threw the book down, seized by fear. How could Southland have known? She searched for answers on the cover, which depicted a cluster of children clenched in a giant, bone-white hand. They were all screaming, and vapor from their mouths spelled out the title, *Book of Screams*.

Book of Dreams was more like it.

But how?

Tanya tried to remember, but everything around the dream was kind of foggy at the edges. She'd forgotten everything about the dream until now, until the story jogged her memory. Until—

Memory flashed.

Tanya leaped off the bed and went to her bookshelf. Eyeing the titles on the creased spines, she fished out volume four of *Stories to Melt Your Mind*, the book in which she'd placed the bookmark, and pulled it out.

Tanya stared at the bookmark. Southland had given it to her several months back, when he'd visited the school.

It had been signed. She'd seen the signature, taken it home with her. She'd forgotten about it all this time.

But the bookmark was blank. Just a slip of cardboard with Southland's name and the book cover on it.

No, Tanya realized. This was not right. The ink had come alive, had come off the page and right onto her.

But the back of the bookmark was just blank cardboard.

She flipped it over, studying the laminated front side with its image of a haunted house, the cover of Southland's book. His name almost glowed in the distinctive red font. Tanya flipped it over again, wondering if there was some kind of trick to it, like Southland had used a disappearing ink.

She ran her finger over the surface, wondering if she'd pick up some trace of the ink, but her fingertips yielded no new surprises.

Her head felt foggy.

Normally she remembered her dreams as soon as she woke. Sometimes she would write them down in a dream journal. The funny thing was, she knew she'd dreamed, but the details wouldn't come.

Tanya shrugged and read on.

THE TAR

Benjamin's newest birthday present was expensive, and according to his parents, he was not meant to play with it often, if at all.

It was one of those flying drones that you could manipulate to move up and down and from side to side. It was way better than the kite Benjamin used to have when he was a little kid. You had to *work* to get a kite up in the air, but a drone? Touch a button, and the sky was the limit.

It wasn't long before Benjamin was able to connect a camera to the bottom of the drone, so that when he flew it up in the air, it could give him an aerial shot of whatever it was hovering above. From his base out in the backyard, Benjamin could control the movements of the drone, sending it over the tall cedar trees lining the fence and up into the air high above. From here he could watch the footage on his laptop computer, *last year's* birthday's present.

For a while he amused himself with images from above. He could see details in the treetops that he'd never noticed before, like the nests of birds, or, if he moved the drone just a bit higher into the sky, details from other people's back-yards.

Wow, the Smiths next door had already opened up their pool! Mrs. Smith was busy swimming lengths back and forth, making big, heavy splashes. She stopped her swimming and looked up at the drone hovering above her, then shook her fist angrily.

Benjamin smiled. *Ha-ha!* He was the king of his domain from here. He could move the drone around and see what everybody within its 500-yard radius was up to.

He pushed the drone around the neighborhood, pre-tending he was in some remote army bunker buried under Washington, DC. At the press of a button, he would deploy his arsenal of weaponry and destroy whatever he saw fit.

"What are you doing, Benjamin?" his mom called from inside.

"Just playing with my birthday present," he said, turning to her.

"Oh," he heard her say from behind the screen door. "Glad you're enjoying it!"

He heard nothing further from her as he continued to push the drone around, seeing how high it could go before he got a warning signal on his computer that he was pushing the drone to its limits.

Once he'd exhausted these opportunities, he wondered where else to take it. What was worth spying on in the surround-ing yards?

Benjamin stood up, tracing a mental map of the area around him. The strip mall was at least a mile or two down the road. The ravine was close by, but the treetops wouldn't yield anything of interest. In fact, the only big building in walking distance he could think of was the school.

"Hey," he said to himself, chewing on the idea. He'd never seen the roof of the school before. The caretakers were the only people who ever went up there—didn't there used to be two? Now it was just Mr. Erikson. As far as Benjamin was concerned, the school rooftop was up there with the far reaches of space and the depths of the Mariana Trench as a region that only an elite few could explore.

Until now.

Benjamin adjusted the controls of the drone, piloting it back up into the air, past his backyard, across two streets and over the fence separating the road from the expanse of the schoolyard. He pushed the drone higher into the air, so that his view of the schoolyard almost resembled the one from Google Maps that his teacher, Mr. Barry, had shown the class for their cartography assignment.

He pushed the drone farther across the field, and the rectangular outline of his bird's-eye view of the school loomed into view on his laptop monitor.

Then a warning light appeared on his controls. He was near the end of the drone's range. Benjamin bit his lip. He wouldn't be able to pilot the drone all the way to the other side of the school, but if he pushed it up a bit higher, the field of view might widen to include the whole rooftop.

He activated the controls and the drone went up, allowing him a better perspective.

Sure enough, he began to see several colored balls dotting the gray surface, presumably ones that had been kicked up there and left to bake in the sun.

He remembered that time back in second grade when he'd been bouncing one of those rubber Super Balls from the vending machine, and after, like, six bounces, it had cleared the top of the school, never to be seen again.

Heck, for all Benjamin knew, it was still there now.

He tried to recall where he'd been playing all those years ago. Was it toward the side of the school in the drone's range?

"Yes," he found himself saying. It was amazing that he could remember an isolated incident like this but not important information that Mr. Barry might want him to regurgitate on a test, or the list of chores his parents gave him on a weekly basis.

He pushed the drone closer to the spot where he'd lost the ball all those years ago. It had been bright red. It would surely be seen amid the litter on the dull gray of the rooftop.

The drone was still quite high in the air, not low enough to pick up any minute details. He'd begun to lower it, so it was hovering closer to the rough gravel covering most of the rooftop, when he spied a flash of something white. Something long and jagged…

"No," he said to himself as he quickly lost sight of the object.

He backed up the drone, trying to find it again.

Benjamin squinted at the image on his laptop. He leaned in closer. There was something lying on the roof of the school. It wasn't one of the soccer balls that had been kicked up there and left forgotten. It wasn't even that red bouncy ball he'd lost years ago. It wasn't the gravel or sticky tar that coated the rooftop. It was something different. Something white. Something that looked almost…human.

What *was* it?

He shook his head. It couldn't be. Was there someone on the roof? A caretaker maybe? But it was Sunday.

And besides, the thing on the roof wasn't moving. It couldn't be a person!

Benjamin strained to get a better look. He had to bring the drone down even closer to get the detail he wanted.

The drone roved over the rooftop, showing old food wrappers and stray leaves and splotches of tar. But there was no large white object. Nothing he could see from this angle anyway.

Maybe if he floated the drone farther up into the air and got yet another high-angle view, he could locate the object and then zoom back in.

Benjamin made a move to raise the drone, but it remained in place.

"C'mon," he grunted, fiddling with the controls. "Just a better view." He could take a snapshot on his computer monitor. That's all he needed, if only he could get some distance between the drone and the rooftop. But the device wasn't moving up. It wasn't even veering left or right. And then Benjamin's controller sent out another warning beep.

This time Benjamin looked at the screen. He saw rooftop gravel rushing up toward him and—

"No!" Benjamin growled, clenching his fists into tight balls. He was about to pound the laptop, but that would be two pieces of equipment destroyed.

Already the truth was dawning on him. He'd lost the drone to the school rooftop.

The very expensive birthday present he was supposed to take care of.

"Benjamin, time for lunch," a voice called from inside.

Benjamin snapped his laptop shut. *Cripes!* He was going to get it now. His parents had just given that drone to him on Friday, and he'd lost it already?

Oh, he was *going* to get it.

Unless…

Unless he could get up there somehow and find it.

He could do it tomorrow, after school, when there would be few people to spot him.

For the moment, in front of his parents, Benjamin could pretend to have lost interest in the drone momentarily and feign excitement about a bike ride outside. That would take him to Monday, and by the end of the day, he'd have the drone back.

Getting to the rooftop wasn't going to be easy, though. Maybe he could hide in the bathroom stall or something while all the other kids left. He knew that Mr. Erikson would be on his rounds, cleaning up the classrooms.

Benjamin would have to swipe the keys off the cart of cleaning supplies Mr. Erikson wheeled around. He could do that when the caretaker was in one of the rooms wiping down the desks. He probably wouldn't even notice the keys were missing, because most of the teachers kept their rooms open after school, and that would give Benjamin time to get to the metal ladder that led up to the hatch by the rooftop. He'd find the key to open the lock, then pocket it.

He would completely ignore the *NO ADMITTANCE—DANGER* sign on the hatch, push it open and get an awesome view from up there. Finding the drone would be easy because it was big and gray and he knew exactly where it had landed.

So on second thought, this *was* pretty darn easy.

A few minutes later Benjamin found himself on the ladder, keys in hand. It did take a few tries before he found the right key for the lock, but once he did, it snapped open. Benjamin pocketed the key. Now he just had to get the hatch open.

That was more of a trick.

For one thing, the hatch was heavy, and Benjamin was weak.

He tried heaving on it first with big heavy pushes, but that just got him tired and upset. So he put his shoulders against the hatch and started to walk up the ladder, using his weight and legs to do the pushing. Benjamin pushed with his shoulders, heaving on the hatch with all of his weight, until finally the heavy door flipped over with a loud clang. Benjamin gave a satisfied smile.

He wouldn't have long, but he didn't need much time.

He pulled himself up and through the open hatch, and swung around to touch down on the gravel of the rooftop. In front of him was a wide, flat expanse, dotted with several chimney vents that belched steam from exhausts elsewhere in the building. Beyond he saw the rooftops of nearby houses.

He focused on scanning for his prize.

There. At the far end of the rooftop, hidden under a clump of leaves, was the drone.

Benjamin wasted no time. He dashed past the deflated soccer balls and dirt-brown tennis balls, his feet crunching over the gravel until he was nearly at the edge of the roof. Benjamin peered over the precipice and felt a wave of dizziness as he saw the pavement two stories down. He held his hands out to steady himself, then crouched to retrieve his prize. *Got it!*

"What are you doing there?" a voice called out from behind.

Benjamin turned to see a lanky, bearded man in torn coveralls, the kind of man he'd normally steer clear of on the street. Mr. Erikson, the caretaker, had followed him up here.

"Uh…" Benjamin began, trying to think of an excuse.

"Did you take my keys?"

"Uh…"

"To get up here?"

"Uh…"

Mr. Erikson shook his head. "All those hours learning in this place, and you only have one-word answers? Technically *uh* isn't even a word, kid."

"Uh…sorry?"

Mr. Erikson fixed Benjamin with a steely gaze.

"Uh…sorry, *Mr. Erikson*," Benjamin said.

"Why are you here?"

"I had to get my drone." Benjamin held it up to show that he wasn't lying.

"You could have asked."

"You would have said no."

Mr. Erikson considered this. "It's a long drop to the pavement."

"I know. But I'm being careful. I won't go over the edge."

"Kid," Mr. Erikson started, then paused. "What's your name?"

"Benjamin."

"Benjamin, listen to me. Listen very carefully. You're in a lot of danger."

"Don't you mean *trouble*?"

"Benjamin, I'm going to ask you to come back here—"

Benjamin lowered his head and sighed. Oh, he was going to get it. First from Mr. Erikson, then his parents, and who knew what punishment each was going to dole out? He took a step forward, and—

"STOP!"

Benjamin looked up. Mr. Erikson was still standing near the hatch. He was holding his hands out so the palms were facing Benjamin. His eyes were wide and fearful.

"I'm not going to fall over the edge, if that's what you're worried about."

"That's *not* what I'm worried about, kid."

"It's Benjamin."

"Don't take another step forward, Benjamin."

Benjamin stopped. He looked down. He was about to step onto tarry blacktop. He didn't understand. He'd walked across it to get this far. But he stepped back onto the portion of the roof that was just gravel and regarded Mr. Erikson quizzically. He wasn't sure what to say, but Mr. Erikson didn't seem angry. He seemed scared.

"Okay," Mr. Erikson said. "I don't want you to move until I tell you to. And I'm going to need you to walk along the edge of the rooftop—really carefully. You got it?"

"Yeah," Benjamin said, not sure what Mr. Erikson was going on about.

"This is the most important part. You hearing me, Ben?"

"It's Benjamin."

"DON'T STEP IN THE TAR."

A cool breeze blew across the rooftop. Benjamin looked down at the tar that had been spread across the roof. Most of the roof was covered in it now. There was only a narrow pathway of gravel along the edges where Benjamin was currently standing, stupidly clutching his drone to his chest, that led around the rooftop. It reminded him of those games he used to play as a little kid, when you pretended that only a few objects around you were safe, and the rest of the ground was lava that would burn you to a crisp.

"What happens if I step in the tar?"

"Don't step in the tar, whatever you do," Mr. Erikson repeated, looking away from Benjamin and at the roof around him. "I don't think you woke it up."

Benjamin decided it was best not to ask about the tar and just pretend it was red-hot lava. He'd played the lava game before—he could play it again.

Slowly, carefully, Benjamin edged along the narrow strip of roof where he didn't see the black tar.

It took him a few minutes to reach the far corner of the roof. In the distance he could see houses and streets. He turned to Mr. Erikson, who was still standing by the open hatch. It seemed like the only exit—but wait. "What if we call the fire department? They can get a ladder up here, right?"

"There isn't enough time," Mr. Erikson said, and now Benjamin noticed that Mr. Erikson wasn't looking in Benjamin's direction. He was looking at a patch of roof somewhere in the open space between them.

Benjamin tried to follow Mr. Erikson's sight line. "Don't look there," Mr. Erikson snapped, but it was too late.

Benjamin saw.

He *had* been right when he got that first view on his laptop screen.

There was the white object he'd seen. It had disappeared from view, but now it was back. It was moving in the tar.

It was a hand.

A hand without skin.

Just the bones, not quite white because there was still some connective tissue holding the individual bones together, and they were also stained from the tar.

But the hand was moving.

Why was it moving?!

Benjamin stood there, dumbfounded, not quite believing what he was seeing.

"Ben," he heard a voice calling to him.

Benjamin snapped himself out of his thoughts. "It's Benjamin," he told Mr. Erikson.

"You've got to keep moving," the caretaker said urgently.

Benjamin nodded. The hand was moving toward him. That wasn't right. Hands couldn't move by themselves. Not dead hands. Not hands disconnected from the rest of their body.

Then Benjamin got it. It wasn't the hand that was moving. The hand was still stuck in the tar.

The *tar* was coming toward him.

He looked down, and he could see the tar pushing forward, lifting up off the roof so that little black tendrils were poking into the air. Trying to feel him out.

In his panic he dropped the drone right into the tar, and the tar raged around it, boiling like a frothing river, swallowing it up in one gulp.

That's when Benjamin screamed.

"Go. NOW!" hollered Mr. Erikson.

Ben had lost the drone, but it had confused the tar. It was still rippling around the inedible piece of metal and plastic. Trying to figure out where the flesh was. Trying to pull at it, dissolve it even.

A moment later Benjamin saw the tar pull away from the drone. It was bent out of shape, the propellers snapped in pieces, the plastic casing warped like it had been stuck in an oven.

Benjamin stared at it in horror.

"RUN!" screamed Mr. Erikson.

Benjamin was not an active kid by any means. The others in his class often made fun of him for his lack of physical ability. He'd always been the last one chosen to join pickup sports games outside at recess, if he was picked at all. He often felt pretty useless.

He wasn't going to be useless now.

He ran.

He stared at the narrow strip of untarred rooftop, stretching in a wavy line along the edge of the roof. It was growing narrower and narrower.

Benjamin jumped up onto the raised metal edge of the roof. He held his breath. One false step, and he'd plummet to the ground below. He held his hands out for balance, like a tightrope walker might. He sucked in gulps of air, trying to keep alert.

Meanwhile, out of the corner of his eye, Benjamin could see the tar moving.

It had followed him. Maybe it could see. Maybe it couldn't. But Benjamin was pretty sure it could feel his movements. It knew its prey was within reach. He watched as the tar thickened in front of him. It had been spread so thin on the roof, but now it was pulling itself into something bigger. Thicker. With greater substance.

And it was growing.

The tar stretched itself into a shape. Bits of gravel and candy wrappers and even a few stray tennis balls were stuck to its surface, but even they moved around as the tar pulled and pushed itself like a ball of taffy. Benjamin could see how unlike tar it was. The black, shimmering surface of the oozing substance was too shiny, too malleable. Benjamin didn't know what it was or how it had gotten here. Nobody was allowed on the roof, and now he knew why.

The tar had become a large misshapen mound. It was rising up past the lip of the roof edge. It was growing taller. Snaky tendrils began to push out of it. Trying to reach him. Trying to grab him.

And then Benjamin saw something large and white push out of the tar and move toward him.

It was a human skull.

Benjamin screamed again. Tried to take a step forward, but the tar followed his movements. Took a step back. No luck. He just stood there, balancing on the edge of the roof. He whimpered.

Then...

"BENJAMIN, RUN!"

In a flash the tar retracted into a liquid puddle, with such speed that the skull popped out of the mound and hung suspended in the air for a moment before splashing back into the pool of black ooze.

The tar moved away from him.

Benjamin looked up.

It was Mr. Erikson. He was stamping his feet and waving his arms and looking with horror right into Benjamin's eyes. "BENJAMIN, YOU'VE GOT TO RUN!!!"

Benjamin jumped off the ledge and back onto the roof. The tar was moving toward Mr. Erikson, who had stepped away from the hatch. He was skirting around it, luring the tar his way to distract it.

Benjamin looked down and saw he had some clearance now. He didn't waste any time. He sprinted toward the open hatch.

It was still several yards away. He could make it, though. As long as he ran and didn't stop or trip or—

His foot caught on something. He pitched forward. He felt his chest hit the jagged gravel. Felt the wind pulled from his lungs. Felt the sting of gravel on his hands, his cheeks. He weakly managed to look back.

He'd tripped on the rib cage of the tar's other victim.

Benjamin screamed again, or tried to, but he was out of breath. Feverishly he sucked the air back into his lungs and tried to pull himself up off the gravel.

He looked around frantically. Where was the tar?

Shaking, he got back to his feet, still searching the roof in bursts so quick it was a wonder he could take anything in. Then, farther away, he saw.

Mr. Erikson was backed up against the edge of the rooftop.

The tar was oozing all around him.

Benjamin saw the look of horror on Mr. Erikson's face. Saw the inky black tendrils push out of the steadily growing mound and then latch on to Mr. Erikson's feet.

Mr. Erikson opened his mouth to scream, but the tar yanked him off his feet, taking the very breath from his throat before he could utter a sound.

Then Mr. Erikson was splayed on the roof, his arm desperately clawing over the edge, and the tar was upon him. He opened his mouth again. "BEENNNNNNN—" he started, but his cry turned to an agonized gurgle as the tar flowed over him like a wave.

Benjamin didn't scream this time. He was running for the hatch.

A few more steps. He could do it.

But the tar was already thinning out, flowing toward him.

Benjamin jumped for it. He grabbed hold of the hatch, pulling himself toward the ladder. Something latched on to his foot. He pulled harder. No. The tar wouldn't have him too.

Benjamin kicked, felt his shoe come off, and he was free! He slammed the hatch down, so the tar was back up there, trapped. He dug into his pocket, and yes! The key was there.

But the tar was trying to pull the hatch open. Trying to get inside after him.

With one hand holding the hatch shut, Benjamin struggled to click the lock shut, to turn the key and hold it tight.

Then, with the kind of speed that would have made him first pick on any of those recess games, Benjamin clambered down the ladder, landed hard on his feet and found himself back in the school hallway, shivering.

His hands were scraped and covered with cuts and scratches. He could feel a warm trickle running down his forehead and didn't need to look in a mirror to know he was bleeding in several places.

It didn't matter. He was *alive*.

Then the other realization. Mr. Erikson.

And the tar.

He could phone the police. That was the right step. It didn't matter that he'd stolen Mr. Erikson's keys and broken onto the roof. It didn't even matter that his birthday drone was trashed.

The thoughts ran through his head as quickly as he ran back home. He didn't turn back once to stare at the school. Not once to look at the rooftop. To see if there was any sign left of Mr. Erikson dangling over the edge.

That image remained burned in his head as he raced back to his house.

He didn't even stop to take his jacket or remaining shoe off until he was in his bedroom, with the door shut behind him. Then came sobs of horror and relief.

Mr. Erikson was gone. The tar had taken him.

A wave of revulsion came over Benjamin. His stomach spun. He'd never intended this.

Mr. Erikson was gone, and Benjamin was still here.

Tears flowed from his eyes, and ribbons of snot poured from his nose. He wiped his face with a sleeve, and then he slowly took off his dirty jacket, kicked off his shoe and collapsed onto his bed.

Benjamin closed his eyes. He squeezed them shut, trying to will himself to sleep, trying to convince himself that this was all just a terrible dream he was going to wake from.

But after a few moments, he heard a knock on the door, and behind it his mother's muffled voice. "Benjamin, is everything all right?"

Benjamin thought about how to answer her. Call the police? They wouldn't believe his story. And what if they did? What if they opened up the hatch on the roof, what then? They'd find Mr. Erikson, but the tar would find them. It would come back down through the hatch. Come after the police, after him.

"I'm okay," he called weakly.

"All right, honey," she said, her voice quieter. "I'm just making supper."

He heard her footsteps thump away, and then he was alone again.

He was going to have to get up and shower. He'd come into the house so quickly that his mother hadn't even seen him or the cuts and blood. He would have to explain. She'd demand it. The more Benjamin thought about it, the more he realized he was going to have to say *something*. When Mr. Erikson failed to show up at work, they were going to check the school cameras. They were going to find him and Mr. Erikson in the hallway. They were going to ask questions.

Benjamin exhaled.

He got up off the bed to go and clean himself up.

Then he stopped.

He saw it.

There, on the bottom of his shoe. Stuck to the sole.

It was only a dark splotch, but it was already oozing.

Benjamin froze. He could only watch as the tar pulled away from his shoe, poked out a tiny little tendril and disappeared into the thick fibers of his bedroom carpet.

He stood there, too afraid to move. To even breathe.

Because now the entire floor was lava.

DUST
TO DUST

Talia's phone buzzed to life. She dug into her pocket and fished it out. She didn't recognize the number, but who knew—maybe it was important. She answered the call and held the phone to her ear. "Hello?"

There was a burst of static on the line. Static, then silence.

"Hello?"

Talia was about to hang up when she heard a voice. The speaker sounded far away, and she had an accent Talia couldn't place. "Hello, ma'am. How are you?"

"Who is this?" Talia said.

"Air-duct cleaning service. Do you need your air ducts cleaned? We can offer you a competitive price—"

Talia scowled. "I told you guys before to stop calling me. You call all the time. We never say yes!" Then she hung up the phone. At first she'd tried to be polite with the air-duct cleaning company. She'd told them she was only a kid and that she wasn't the one to talk to about this kind of stuff.

Of course, they called again.

Not right away, mind you, and not from the same number.

But every few weeks, when Talia was at home trying to accomplish something important, like getting to the final confrontation in the video game she'd been mastering for the last few months, the phone would ring and break her concentration. "Air-duct cleaning service—"

"Shove it!" Talia had said the last time, hanging up the phone and losing her game.

And now they were back again.

Did these guys just sit there at a call center, punching in various digits and waiting to see who answered?

The more Talia thought about it, the stranger it seemed. Who even took a job at that call center? The workday must be terrible, having to deal with angry people on their phones yelling or swearing or hanging up on them.

And what about the callers who actually wanted their air ducts cleaned?

Did these guys come straight to your house? Were they actually any good at cleaning air ducts? Talia wondered how effective this company was if they spent what seemed to be an eternity phoning people, trying to drum up business. Couldn't you just go online and find a local air-duct cleaning service with a good rating? Why would anyone ever hire the weird company known for its random phone calls?

Then Talia realized she was giving this waaaaay too much thought.

Besides, she had a video game to master, and nobody was going to break her concentration tonight.

It was at that point that she unpaused the game and was soundly defeated by the evil alien overlords from level twenty-eight.

"GAAAH!" Talia screamed, hurling her controller at the floor.

It wasn't the phone that woke Talia up.

She lay there in bed, eyes open. Moonlight spilled into her room through a gap in the curtains. She breathed heavily, trying to calm herself down. She was sweating. Why was she sweating so much? Was it a nightmare? Talia hadn't had one of those in some time.

Still, her whole bed was soaked in sweat. Talia sat up, and she could feel the sweat gluing her pajama top to her back.

The room was piping hot. Hadn't her mom set the thermostat properly? Wasn't she getting enough air-conditioning from her vent? Her mom had told Talia to shut the window so she could run the AC, but she must have forgotten to turn it on.

Talia slipped out of bed and went to put her hand above the vent in the corner of the room.

Normally there'd be a refreshing gasp of cool air coming through, but tonight? Nothing.

Talia lifted the vent cover off, revealing a dark hole within. Taking care not to cut her hand on the sharp metal edges, she tried to feel inside for any suggestion that the air conditioner was working.

Nope.

Talia shrugged and went to place the vent cover back on when—

Talia.

She sat there, not quite sure what to make of the breathy sound she'd heard. It was just two syllables. Maybe not a word, really. Not her name, of all things—

Talia.

Crap, maybe she was having a nightmare after all! She slapped her cheek to try to wake herself up. Nothing changed.

The sound was coming from down there in the pipes. Talia leaned forward, trying to hear it again. It was probably just that—the pipes. Or, better still, the air-conditioning was trying to kick into gear and pump some cool air into her room at last. That actually made sense, not some crazy idea that a voice coming through the vent was saying her name.

Talia! I'm down here!

Talia screamed and bolted away from the vent.

She sat on the carpet, breathing heavily. Waiting.

When she heard the voice again, it had an even more distant timbre, like it had moved farther down along the pipes. The voice sounded strained, in discomfort or even pain.

It was definitely moving. Talia got onto her knees, now over the initial shock. Whatever was making the sound was farther away now, the voice shifting and getting more muted and muffled. Talia tracked the sound with her eyes, following where she thought the vent led, across the length of her room.

The thing in the pipes was leaving the room, going down the hall.

Talia opened the door and tiptoed into the hallway.

She stopped, straining to hear the sound. For a second she thought she'd lost it, but there it was, at the very edge of her hearing. Muted, pleading. *Talia! Talia, come help me!*

Still in the pipes.

And then Talia realized. Not the pipes.

"The air ducts," she whispered.

There was a larger grille mounted on the wall, just above the baseboard. Talia bent down and put her ear to the grille. "Are you still there?" she asked.

"Talia," the voice answered back, "is that really *you*?"

Talia gulped. She stood up. This was wrong. This was not cool. This was definitely something worth waking up her parents for. She took a few steps back.

"Don't do it," the voice called out.

Talia stopped again. "Do what?"

"You're going to tell your parents. Not a good idea. They won't believe you."

They will if I show you to them, Talia thought. And the only way to do that was to open up that grille and find whoever was talking to her.

Talia got up and doubled back to the bathroom, where her parents kept a few random tools under the sink for emergencies. There was the screwdriver. Talia snatched it up and was about to leave when she thought about the voice. It seemed like it needed help, but what if it *didn't*? She pulled out the hammer too. Just in case.

But…there was something familiar about the voice that Talia couldn't place, something in the way it pleaded that was slipping past her reservations. Something that seemed to egg Talia on to get the job done, to rip off the grille and see what was inside.

She stepped back into the hallway.

"Talia, what are you doing?" the voice asked.

"I'm coming to get you out of there," Talia said.

She thought about this. It would be dark in the ducts. She'd need a light—like the one on her phone. Talia went and got it, slipped it into the flimsy pocket of her pajama pants, returned to the hallway and set to work. She started to unscrew the grille. It was bigger than the vent cover in her bedroom. Big enough that she could stick her whole head in the hole behind it, maybe even her shoulders and arms too.

Clink! One of the screws plunked to the wooden floor.

"How did you even get in there?" Talia wondered aloud. She thought of the time she was fooling around at the community center and her friend Jiro stuffed her into one of the lockers. It was a tight fit. Talia couldn't move, and she'd panicked at the thought of being trapped there. So how did whoever was in the duct get there in the first place? And why wasn't she freaking out?

And, most naggingly, why was her voice so familiar?

Clink! Another screw came loose.

Talia strained to see into the inky darkness behind the grille. Was the owner of the voice just beyond it? Or trapped deeper within?

Talia stopped. "Did you hear me? How did you get in there? A person can't just accidentally end up in the ducts."

Nothing.

Then: "Come on, hurry up. I can't stay trapped in here much longer."

Of course, Talia knew she should stop. She'd known since first hearing the voice that this was something she shouldn't be doing by herself in the middle of the night.

Clink!

The grille swung down and thunked against the floor, held to the wall by a solitary screw on the top left. Talia stopped, staring at the sliver of darkness that was revealed. She aimed the light of her phone's screen into the dark void beyond, straining to see. Straining to hear…

"TALIA!!!!" The voice seemed only inches away from her. Talia jumped back.

"Sorry, I'm sorry," the voice said again. It was so familiar. Talia couldn't put her finger on where she'd heard it before. But she was compelled to see this one through.

Fighting past the fear that held her back, Talia reached forward, unfastened the final screw and pulled away the grille in one swift movement.

"There, it's done! You're free!" Talia said, and she even managed a smile.

No response.

"I mean, if you got in, then I guess this is how you get out, right? Can you see the light? I've got the grille off."

But there was no voice.

Of course there was no voice. Talia had stayed up too late. This had all been in her head. There were no people trapped in ducts in houses. That was scary crap she'd seen in a gazillion horror movies on Netflix.

She'd woken herself up and pulled the grille off for no reason. She was about to put it back on, screw it back in, when—

Talia!

She wasn't sure if the voice was coming from deep within the duct or from her own mind.

Talia!

But the voice was fading. Like it was being pulled back into the duct, back toward the furnace or the air-conditioning unit, wherever it was the duct led.

Talia sat there and decided.

In one hand she clutched the hammer, and in the other, her phone. She turned the flashlight back on. A powerful LED beam burst out into the dark around her. Carefully, quietly, she extended the light into the duct.

The weight of her hand pressed down against the cool metal, causing the phone to clunk and echo.

Talia stared deep into the duct. There was nothing there but empty space and cobwebs and dust.

Lots of dust.

"Ugh," Talia said. Maybe they did need their air ducts cleaned after all. She knew that dogs and cats shed and got their hair all over the place, but Talia's family didn't have pets, so this wasn't pet hair. It was regular old dust, and lots of it, piled up into the corners. And what was dust? Bits and pieces of things from around the house.

And human skin.

Talia remembered learning this in a science class, that most of the dust we see is really just shed bits and particles of human skin. Gross.

She leaned in farther, this time bringing in the hand with the hammer, and inched forward so that her head was swallowed up by the duct.

Talia could hear the thrum of the blood pumping through the veins in her neck and ears.

She shone the light around, but there was nothing there. No voice, no person, no thing.

Just dust.

"Hello?" she called out, one last time to give it one more chance, to be absolutely sure that all of this was just in her head.

And then, from down there, in the darkness:

You came.

Talia gasped.

I knew you would.

This time the voice didn't sound remotely worried. It was pleased.

Talia tried to wriggle her head out of the duct, but she was stuck.

"Crap," she hissed under her breath.

It was only a matter of time, the voice said. Talia still wasn't sure if she was imagining it, but it was getting louder. She heard something shifting around a corner of the duct. She didn't want to see it. She just wanted to get out of there. She opened her mouth to scream. She took a breath and then—

The dust shifted, as if caught in the draft of her own inhalation.

Some of the dust went straight into her mouth. Talia choked on it. And the dust was filling up the whole duct now. Clouds and clouds of it!

Something was pushing its way up through the duct, coming for her, pushing all the dust out of the depths and into her face.

Talia coughed, but even with the light on, she couldn't see anything but dust.

BUZZZZZ.

Talia gasped again, choking again on the dust. It was her phone! Who was calling at this time of night?

Didn't matter. She flipped it on involuntarily, and before she could even answer, Talia heard the familiar voice. "Air-duct cleaning service. Do you need your air ducts cleaned? We can offer you a competitive price—"

"YES, YES!! Please get over here right away!!!"

"As you wish, ma'am."

The phone clicked off before she could give them her address. Anyway, they wouldn't be able to come till the morning. Talia struggled to pull herself free. She opened her mouth to scream for her parents. "Mom! Dad!"

She wondered if they could even hear her with her head stuck in the duct. Why were they still asleep in their beds? Hadn't they heard the commotion?

Talia heard a door open behind her.

Phew! It must be her parents. Thank goodness they were here. They'd just give her a hefty pull, and this whole mess would be sorted out.

Talia felt a pair of hands clasp her ankles and yank her backward.

And then her head was out, and she was gasping and coughing on the floor. She couldn't see at first because so much dust had covered her face, getting in her ears and mouth and nose and eyes. She wiped it away, straining to see through the thick tears pouring out of her eyes and down her cheeks. She blinked, but things were still not in focus yet. All Talia could taste were the salty tears and her own snot.

Talia blinked, and the world came back into focus.

Not her parents.

There were two men standing over her, each holding powerful flashlights. They were dressed in coveralls from head to toe. They had backpacks strapped on that looked more like portable vacuum cleaners.

One of them reached a free hand down to Talia. She took it and let him hoist her to her feet.

Talia just stood there shivering in the hallway. The hammer was on the floor where she'd dropped it, just out of reach. "Who are you? What are you doing here?"

The two men looked at each other and smiled. "Air-duct cleaning service," one of the men said. "You wanted your air ducts cleaned, didn't you?"

Talia shook her head. "What? It's the middle of the night! How did you guys get in here?" Her mind flooded with questions. "How did you even know where to come?"

The other man pointed to Talia's phone lying on the floor, still sending a beam of light into the air, where the clouds of dust could be seen whirling and spinning. "We tracked your phone. We're very efficient."

"But...but you called, like, a minute ago."

"We're *very* efficient," the other man said.

But they weren't paying too much attention to Talia. They were fiddling with the vaccuums strapped to their backs. Large, thick hoses jutted out of the packs, which they held in their hands. One of the men flipped on a switch, and Talia felt a huge rush of air in the hallway.

"You're cleaning the ducts?"

"Yes," the man said. "There was some debris in there, but I can see we've cleared it out."

Talia shook her head. "No, you don't understand. There's something trapped down there. Something in the dust."

Involuntarily, Talia stepped closer to the men. She felt her clothes pulling away, sucked by the force of the vacuums.

The suction pulled at her chest and arms. Her long hair whipped toward the men and their machines. "Hey, can you turn those things off?" she said, pointing to the hose of the closest vacuum. "They're really strong."

"Oh yes," said the man, his voice barely audible over the roar of the vacuum. "They need to be, for what we do."

But the two men weren't even going near the duct. Talia felt herself getting yanked forward from the force of the vacuums, until she stood right over the open end of the hose.

The vacuum didn't stop. The powerful suction kept tugging at her shirt and at her body.

Talia tried to pull herself free. "Hey, come on. Quit it!"

But the men said nothing. Not even as Talia screamed out in pain as the vacuum sucked at her skin too. Pulling and wrenching her back, pulling parts of her *into* the hose.

She could feel her body bending under the pressure, feel the flesh and bone getting sucked down the hose. There was no way she'd even fit in there, but the machine had power. So. Much. Power!

Talia whimpered, feeling her arms and legs fold up with crispy snapping sounds. All she could do was stare ahead at the cloud of dust illuminated by the light from her phone.

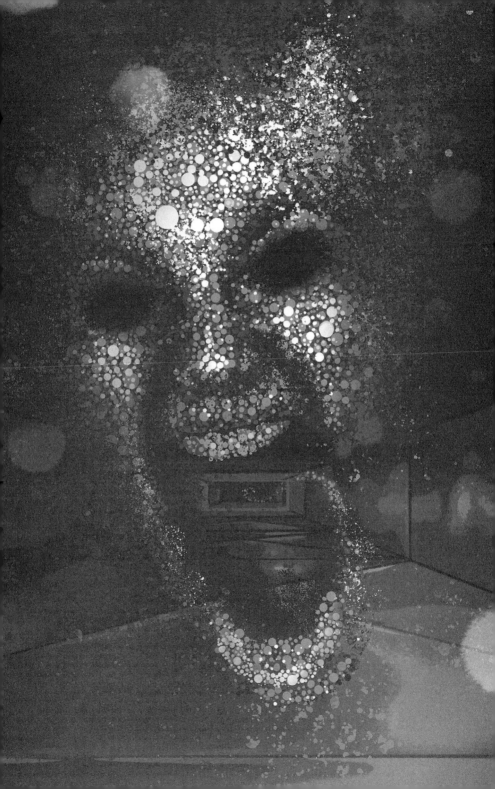

The cloud turned and twisted, and for a second Talia thought she could see it forming a ghostly shape. *Her* shape. With *her* face.

The cloud of dust looked right into Talia's face and smiled.

"Talia," a voice said.

Talia realized it was her own.

Saying nothing else, the air-duct cleaners got on with their work.

And all was quiet once again in the house.

part three

"You're here to see him, aren't you? Joel Southland."

Tanya nodded slowly. There were already a few people milling about the library, clutching books to their chests and not examining the ones on the shelves. This girl was shorter and younger than Tanya. She had olive skin and dark, curly hair. Three well-read copies of Joel Southland books were in her hands. She rocked back and forth excitedly. "I hear he's an amazing speaker."

"Yeah," Tanya said, looking past her over to where the librarian had set up several rows of chairs in a cleared-out spot of the library.

The girl thrust a hand in Tanya's direction. "I'm Cindy, by the way."

"Tanya."

"You're not from around here."

"I'm visiting my grandmother for the week," Tanya said.

"You visit your *grandma* for spring break?"

That part was true—Tanya *was* visiting her grandmother. She was pretty strict, and she didn't have Wi-Fi, so these visits weren't Tanya's idea of a good time. But when Tanya had learned that Joel Southland was going to be making a library visit to her grandmother's town, she'd jumped at the chance to find out more about what was going on.

"So what's your favorite? *Book of Screams? Tales to Make Your Eyeballs Explode? Gut Wrenchers?* I like *Gut Wrenchers.*"

Tanya turned her attention away from the space where Southland was going to appear and back to Cindy. "Oh, can you really choose a favorite?" If Tanya had been pressed a few months ago, that would have been a real answer. But now she couldn't bear to look at his stories. How had he stolen her nightmare? It was worded so clearly, every last scrap of detail extracted from her mind and put into words. She didn't think she would ever read anything by Joel Southland again.

But she had a job to do.

"Look, he's here!"

Tanya could hear squeals of delight tearing through the people who had gathered. She felt Cindy's hand clasp her wrist. "Come on. Let's get a good seat before they're gone."

But Tanya pulled away. "You go ahead. I'll find my own seat."

Cindy shrugged. "Whatever. Just trying to be friendly."

Before Tanya could say anything, Cindy turned and ran toward the front row of seats. Other kids were making a break to do the same.

Tanya held back, far enough away that she wouldn't be noticed.

"Oh, excuse me."

Tanya felt a tap on her shoulder, but it was the voice that startled her. She knew it immediately, and it was confirmed when she quickly whirled around and found herself staring up at Joel Southland.

He was dressed in his trademark black pants and black shirt. He smiled politely at her.

Tanya opened her mouth to speak, but no sound came.

Did he remember her?

Tanya waited, but he barely even looked at her. His eyes moved past her to the eagerly assembled crowd.

Tanya quickly got out of his way and moved farther away from the others, taking refuge behind a tall bookshelf. Through the gap between the books, Tanya watched as Southland wended his way between the rows of chairs.

Then he went to the podium, opened his laptop, and the screen behind him blazed to life with the blood-red font proclaiming his name.

It was Southland's turn to open his mouth to speak and come up short. He was staring at the space where Tanya had been. She could see the glimmer of recognition in his eyes.

He knew! He *did* remember.

Tanya's heartbeat quickened. Her legs were telling her to run, but she had to see this through. She'd come here to learn more, not to get scared and go skulking back home. She could see Southland scanning the crowd, searching for her.

But he couldn't find her, and eventually he cleared his throat, gave the crowd a confident grin and launched into his book talk.

It was the same presentation, the same old story, the same signed bookmarks.

Tanya watched it all from her hiding place behind the bookshelf. At one point the librarian came up to her, touched her on the shoulder and asked if Tanya wanted to get a closer look.

Tanya shook her head vigorously. "No," she said, almost not daring to speak. "I'm just watching."

"I know," the librarian cooed, casting her eyes over to Southland. "He's quite amazing, isn't he?"

Tanya clenched her teeth. She waited for the presentation to end, waited for Southland to hand out his bookmarks and waited for the kids to clear out.

Cindy was the first to go. She had a silly grin on her face that came from meeting a favorite celebrity. She was staring at the inscription on her bookmark.

There were no adults with her. Tanya followed her out of the library and tapped Cindy's shoulder once they were safely outside. "Cool bookmark," Tanya said. "Can I see what he wrote?"

Cindy spun around. "Oh, it's you."

Tanya reached out for the bookmark. "Here, let me see that."

But Cindy pulled it back. "No way. This one's special. He told me. I was the first one in line, and he used his special author pen, only he ran out of ink so he had to use a regular pen for the others—"

"Cindy, you need to get rid of that thing," Tanya said gravely.

"Nuh-uh."

"It's dangerous."

"You're crazy." Cindy turned and stormed over to a parked car. The side door popped open, and she got inside.

Tanya immediately veered to the bike rack at the side of the library and unlocked her bike. She was going to have to be quick. She got on and pedaled after the car. Tanya desperately hoped that this kid lived nearby, in town. If the car moved too far out of the neighborhood, or onto a faster-moving road, Tanya would be out of luck. As it was, pedaling her bike at even city speeds was tricky after the first few blocks, but at least the streets were full of all-way stops. Tanya had a moment to catch her breath as she tried to stay far enough back that the driver didn't notice her.

Eventually, after meandering through the tree-lined neighborhood, the car pulled into a driveway and came to a stop by a two-story house with a large oak tree beside it. Tanya squeezed on the brakes and planted her feet onto the pavement. She watched as Cindy and her mother headed inside.

She couldn't wait here all afternoon. She'd have to double back to her grandmother's house and let her know she was safe. Really, the only time to come was after her grandmother had nodded off to sleep. Tanya just hoped it wouldn't be too late.

It was a good thing Tanya's grandmother dozed off watching TV. She was the kind of sound sleeper who could pass out on the couch and not get up until morning. Tanya was banking on it, because she didn't want to have to deal with the fallout of sneaking out after dark.

She crept outside, found her bike at the side of the house and pedaled over to Cindy's place. She made sure to put her bike on the other side of the street, in a quiet, dark spot behind some shrubs.

Then it was time to wait.

Tanya had been waiting for forty minutes when she heard a rumble from behind.

A pair of headlights stretched shadows across the pavement.

Tanya crouched and waited for the car to pass. It should have just sailed on down the road, but instead the car came to a deliberate stop at the curb just a house down from Cindy's.

Tanya peered over the top of the bush and felt her heart leap into her throat.

There, in the driver's seat, sat Joel Southland.

He was fiddling with something, but from her distance Tanya could not tell what. She heard the metallic creak of the car door swinging open, saw Southland step out onto the sidewalk and quietly, carefully, pace over to Cindy's house.

Tanya was just in time, but for what exactly? What was Southland up to?

He moved closer to the house and came to a stop behind the big oak tree. Then he waited.

There was no way to figure out what Southland was doing from this far away. Southland's car was just across the street and would provide better cover. Trying to keep a low profile, Tanya got onto her hands and knees and scuttled across the road. She felt the blacktop scrape against her bare elbows, but she clenched her teeth and forced herself to crawl. She huddled against the rear tire, pressing her back against the dirty hubcap. Then she peered over the car to look for Southland.

He had moved away from the tree, and his body was silhouetted against the white siding of the house. He was standing perfectly still and looking up at the windows on the second story.

Only now, as she sat there waiting, did Tanya hear the roar of the crickets and other night insects in her ears. She tried to slow her breathing to calm herself.

How long was he going to stand there?

And what was he going to do?

Maybe waiting was the wrong choice after all.

Maybe she needed to go to the house, knock on the door, wake Cindy. It would stop Southland. He'd know Tanya was onto him, but she'd save this kid from whatever Southland was up to.

Tanya got to her feet, uncertain what choice to make, and then—

A scream cut through the night like a blade. Tanya jumped.

Joel Southland craned his neck toward the sound.

A light flicked on in an upper room, spilling through the night and framing Southland in a yellow square. The light made his eyes glow like an animal's. Southland froze in place, his glance still cast upward. The shades were drawn in the room, but Tanya could hear the muffled sounds of adult voices. And a girl's sobs.

Eventually the voices died down, and the light went back out. The cloak of darkness seemed to magnify the sounds around Tanya—the rustle of leaves in the breeze, the buzzing of crickets and Southland's footsteps moving even closer to the house.

In the dim light it was still difficult to make out much of him other than a slender silhouette. He reached into his pocket and pulled out...something.

She had to get closer.

Taking a breath and trying to calm the mad beating of her heart, Tanya crouched, holding her arms out for balance, and moved away from the relative safety of the car. Several paces

ahead of her was a low wall of shrubbery. She went to duck behind it, but her foot caught a bump in the pavement, and suddenly she felt herself pitching forward onto the concrete. The sudden jolt took the breath out of her, and she gasped for air.

Had he seen? Had he heard?

She waited a minute and then shakily glanced over the top of the shrubs.

Southland was still by the house, but now there was another patch of light, this one focused just below the window.

It was coming from Southland's phone, and he was careful to keep the beam trained away from the glass.

What for?

That's when Tanya saw it.

A flicker of movement just below the window, just where Southland's light was aiming.

Something small.

An animal?

Tanya strained to see it. She pushed away from the safety of the shrub, moving closer. She kept her eyes locked on the small patch of light slowly moving down the white siding of the house. The closer she got, the clearer it became.

It was not an animal she recognized. It was more like the disembodied tentacle of some undersea thing, thinning out, pulling itself forward, running like liquid down the side of the house.

There wasn't much of it—it was about the size and shape of a small child's hand, especially when the liquid ran out in thin, fingerlike tendrils, feeling its way along the edge of the house and sliding downward.

By the time she had moved close enough to get a real good look at it, Southland had blocked her view. He put the phone away, digging into his pocket for something else. For a second, before he switched the light off, Tanya caught a glimpse of the other object.

A glass jar with a screw-top lid.

He held out his hand, and Tanya heard the splash of that liquid something hitting the jar.

Then she turned and ducked behind the rough back of the large oak tree. And she waited, grinding her teeth together.

She heard Southland's feet on the sidewalk, heard the car door creak open, and then she knew it was now or never. Find out what Southland was up to before he drove off into the night again.

She peered around the tree to see Southland sitting in the car. The interior light was on so that he could see inside the vehicle. This meant that (a) Tanya could see Southland, and (b) he could not see clearly into the dark. So Tanya crept closer.

She watched as he reached over to the passenger seat, got a large pad of paper and set it on his lap. Even from this distance, Tanya could see there were no words on the pad. Was this how Southland got his ideas? By setting some kind of weird ink monster loose on kids, getting them to scream in fear and then writing while inspired by their terror?

Southland dipped into his pocket, pulling out the jar. The black liquid sloshed around inside. Slowly, carefully, he unscrewed the lid and then tipped the jar forward, as if to pour it out.

Tanya narrowed her eyes. For what purpose? The ink would spill, the pad would get soiled and—

But the ink didn't *pour* out. Not exactly.

A thin ribbon of ink seemed to wriggle out of the open mouth of the vial and oozed like molasses onto the page.

Tanya could see it clearly because, without realizing it, she had paced closer to the car. She caught herself and froze, but Southland's attention was on the eerie ink. He stared, mesmerized, as it danced over the page, whirling and twirling and smearing itself across the paper.

Moving closer still, Tanya saw the ink. Saw what it was doing. It was *writing*.

She couldn't tell what, though. Her gaze flitted to Southland. His eyes tracked back and forth, reading the page. "Yes," she heard him say, "yes, that's quite good. Quite good indeed."

His breathing grew ragged as the ink continued to ooze from the bottle, creeping over the paper until it had completely filled the top page of the pad.

In one quick movement Southland ripped off the page and gently set it on the passenger seat. Without wasting a beat, he tipped the jar of ink and the writing continued.

Tanya pushed farther forward. She was so close to the truth. She watched as Southland read another page, tore it off the pad and poured out the last of the ink.

"Yes," he said. "That will do nicely."

He reached a hand up and flicked off the interior light of the car.

Southland turned on the engine, the headlights blazing, their reflected glow illuminating Tanya. He looked up and saw her, and Tanya froze.

"You," he said, his expression shifting. "I know you!"

Tanya shook her head, not to disagree with him but to get herself to start moving.

Southland revved the engine, and that was all Tanya needed. She ducked around the other side of the car and dodged across the street, toward the shrub where she'd pitched her bike. She looked over her shoulder and saw Southland rummaging through his stuff in a flurry.

Quickly she picked up the bike. Her legs and arms felt stiff. She tried to get herself balanced, but fear made her lose control for a moment. She planted her feet on the ground and then put one foot on the pedal. She couldn't outrun him, but she could lose him in the neighborhood pathways.

The sound of the engine roared in her ears. Did he mean to run her down?

Tanya turned. There was a blur of motion as the car sped away, and as it passed, she felt something splash against her cheek.

Southland drove off into the night.

As she watched the red glow of his taillights, Tanya sucked in a worried breath and clawed at her cheek. The ink was already working its way up her face, the liquid icy cold. She felt like she was going to faint as it seeped into the corners of her eyes...

SUPPLY AND DEMAND

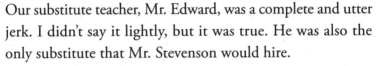

Our substitute teacher, Mr. Edward, was a complete and utter jerk. I didn't say it lightly, but it was true. He was also the only substitute that Mr. Stevenson would hire.

I didn't know why. We kept telling Mr. Stevenson about Mr. Edward. How he shouted and banged his fist on the desk and made us stay in at recess if we got too loud. There was a reason Mr. Edward had never become a real full-time teacher, and it was that he was the *worst*.

Mr. Stevenson was our homeroom teacher. He was the best teacher I'd ever had. Why? He took the time to get to know us. He knew how much I liked science, for example. And building spaceships out of LEGO. He even remembered the details of all the stories he had us write for assignments. And he listened. Whenever there was a fight at recess, he had us sit in a community circle to hear both sides of the problem. Usually we could come to some kind of agreement. Mr. Stevenson got our respect.

What I loved most about Mr. Stevenson was how much he tried to share his passion for science with us. He managed to get the science room for our homeroom. It was the one attached to the giant storage closet where the teachers kept all the old books and science equipment that never got used anymore. There were piles of dusty old encyclopedias but also cool stuff, like a real projector that you could turn on and use to show ancient educational films. Mr. Stevenson showed us one once, and we all laughed at it together.

The room also had equipment from back when our school went all the way up to tenth grade and they'd held high-school science classes here. The shelves had old beakers and Bunsen burners and even some chemicals stored in jars super high up on the shelves. We weren't allowed to touch the chemicals. I didn't think anyone had used them in years. They'd probably all gone bad.

"Why are you looking at the closet door, Robert?"

I shifted my glance from the closet over to the hulking figure of Mr. Edward. He had a smell about him that was hard to ignore. But if you could, you'd get lost in the thick tangle of his beard, which he probably kept to hide his skin, which was red and puffy like it had been soaked in a pickling vat. The whites of his eyes and his teeth had a yellow tinge, and his features were fixed in a permanent scowl. Right now his fists were clenched so tightly that the veins looked like they were going to pop right through the skin.

"I was just thinking of the answer," I muttered, trying to remember the lesson at hand.

SLAM!

I jumped, heart in my throat. Mr. Edward had smacked his fist against the desk with such force that it sounded like a thunderclap. He looked like he wanted to use that fist to pound against something softer than a desk, but I could see him thinking twice. Slowly he let out a long breath and unclenched. "Speak up, Robert," he said at last, breaking the silence. "You know I can't abide mumbles and whispers."

"I-I was thinking of the answer—"

"Too late," he snapped. "I'll make a note of that." Mr. Edward lumbered back to Mr. Stevenson's desk and scribbled something down in a notebook there. If it had been any other substitute teacher, I'd have tried to sneak over and take a look, but I didn't dare do anything with Mr. Edward in sight.

Crap. What kind of notes was he leaving about me now? Mr. Stevenson would see them, and he might not understand.

At first recess I went out to play soccer with Wajahat and Asir. When I went to take a shot, I ended up missing the ball completely and landing on my knee. I landed so hard that the dirt scraped off a layer of skin, and I started gushing blood. The sight of blood gets me screaming, and I totally embarrassed myself in front of everybody. I had to go limping into the school to get some gauze and bandages from the school nurse.

When I'd stopped crying, the nurse sent me back outside. I took my time because my knee still hurt super badly, and also I didn't want to show my face to anyone right away. As I slowly hobbled down the long hallway, I went past our homeroom door.

The blind in its window hadn't been pulled down all the way, and there was a gap where I could see inside.

Mr. Edward was still at the desk, scribbling more notes, and I immediately ducked out of sight. I could hear him muttering under his breath even from out here.

What the heck was he writing now? I was suddenly filled with an urge to snatch the notebook and quickly flip through it.

Through the gap under the blind, I saw Mr. Edward get up and move over to the supply closet.

He turned a key, opened the door and disappeared inside. I could hear clunking and shuffling coming from the closet, like he was moving boxes or breaking things.

He was doing *something* in there, but he definitely wasn't coming out yet.

I checked my phone. Three minutes had gone by and he was still in there, and the cacophony kept on. There was no other way out. I was pretty sure of that. He was clearly doing something that was taking forever.

That's when the thought hit me. With Mr. Edward in the closet, I might have enough time to slip into our homeroom and see what the heck he was scribbling in his notebook. Only a quick glance before he locked it back up in Mr. Stevenson's desk. It would take only seconds, and Mr. Edward was clearly not coming out anytime soon.

I clasped my hand around the door handle and turned it. Quietly I opened the door just enough to get inside.

Heart hammering in my chest, I padded over to the desk. I could hear Mr. Edward in the closet. He was making a lot of noise. I had no idea what he would want in there, and I didn't care. As long as he was doing something, I had a chance to see what he was writing about all of us.

I looked at the notebook, but instead of notes, all I could see were big dark scribble marks. Not words at all.

I blinked. What?

I turned one page back, to the lesson plan for the morning. I scanned the typewritten notes for any mention of my name in the margins, but again, all I could see were huge dark squiggle marks. All over the page. It wasn't any kind of language, just a bunch of doodling. It looked like it had been scribbled firmly, with an angry hand.

I flipped back through a few more pages. Some had Mr. Stevenson's lesson plans in there. Neat and tidy. But other pages were crumpled and torn and full of more scribbles.

I knew they were all from Mr. Edward.

I shook my head. These looked like the scribblings of a wild thing.

Mr. Stevenson must have known about the notes. They were in *his* book of lesson plans. So why keep hiring Mr. Edward?

A shuffling sound came from inside the closet.

Crap!

I moved away from the notebook, turned and strode toward the door. It was only a few paces away, but my knee was hurting from getting skinned. It was slowing me down. If Mr. Edward saw me leaving, I'd be in such trouble—

"Robert!"

I stopped. I turned. I saw.

Impossible.

Mr. *Stevenson* stood before me. He was halfway between the closet and the desk. I could tell he'd come out in a hurry, because he was still in midstride. His shirt was buttoned up the wrong way, and it wasn't tucked in properly the way it usually was. His hand was outstretched toward me.

I froze in place. Mr. Stevenson looked from me to the closet to his desk, where the notebook pages had been turned back several days. I hoped he might not notice that it was open to a different spot but held my gaze on them for too long, because when Mr. Stevenson turned back to me, I could tell he knew I'd seen them. That it was a detail he didn't want others to see. He shifted his weight from foot to foot nervously.

For a moment neither of us spoke, and all to be heard was the ticking of the clock above the door.

Finally he broke the silence. "What did you see?"

"You—you came out of the room," I said, not understanding. "But *Mr. Edward* went in."

I tried to look over his shoulder. Was Mr. Edward there too? How could that be? There was no other way out of that supply closet.

Mr. Stevenson closed the closet door. "Mr. Edward has gone home. I am feeling much, much better now." He paused a moment, and his gaze went back to his desk. "I will take over for the rest of the day. We won't see Mr. Edward again for some time, I should think."

It was only then that I realized he had something in his hand. It was vial of greenish liquid. Shakily he picked it up and put it to his lips, downing the substance quickly.

There was something about the hand holding the vial. It was noticeably bigger than his other one—a mismatch.

Mr. Stevenson let out a cough, like whatever he'd sipped was sour.

I looked at him. "Are you okay?"

He slipped the vial, and his big hand, into his pocket and left them there, hidden.

"Mr. Stevenson?"

Then he burped suddenly and pulled his hand back out, putting it to his mouth.

"Excuse me," he said, but there was a strained look on his face. He put the other hand to his throat and swallowed once, twice. He closed his eyes, then blinked and opened them and stared at me again.

Both hands were the same size again.

"Are you sure you're okay?" I asked.

"Absolutely sure," he said after a moment. He flexed his fingers and slipped both hands into his pockets. As if everything was totally normal.

We were all pleased to see Mr. Stevenson again. Wajahat pumped his fist in the air and cheered, which Mr. Stevenson did not approve of, but we could all see the smile on his face.

He picked up the lesson that Mr. Edward had failed to complete, bringing us down to the carpet to teach. If it were any other teacher, we'd all complain about how sitting on the carpet was for kindergarten kids. Mr. Stevenson had taught kindergarten at his last school, the year before coming to Gilmore P.S., and we just kind of took it in stride, even though with twenty-eight of us sitting cross-legged, there wasn't much carpet space for anyone.

I kept back from my usual spot at the front, settling in near the middle so I could blend in and think. I couldn't figure out how Mr. Stevenson had returned so quickly. How he'd emerged, like magic, from that closet. I had to know.

When the lunch bell finally rang, and we all sat down to eat at our desks, Mr. Stevenson came by before heading off to the staff room. "Hey, Robert. Can you help me clean up some of the art supplies after you're done eating?"

I looked up and nodded. "Sure. Can I see if Wajahat wants to help?"

"Wajahat wants to play soccer," Wajahat said. He liked to talk about himself in the third person, especially when he heard his name being tossed back and forth.

I shrugged. "I guess not."

After the bell rang and everybody put their lunches away, Mr. Stevenson returned as everyone spilled out of the room. I held back, until it was just the two of us left. He told me to wait at the door. Then he went into the room and emerged a little bit later with some papers tucked under his arm.

"Just wait here a moment. I won't be long. I need to deliver these down to Mrs. Watson."

I watched Mr. Stevenson stride off down the hall. Once he was out of sight, I went back inside. The notebook of lesson plans was gone, locked up in his desk.

I had a feeling the supply closet would be locked as well, but when I put my hand on the doorknob, it turned without a problem.

Had Mr. Stevenson forgotten to lock it when we'd met at first recess? It was likely. I'd caught him off guard.

It was ridiculous, but I had to get to the bottom of this. Mr. Edward had been in here. He'd gone in, but he hadn't come back out. At the back of my mind, I wondered, Was he still in there?

I opened the door and stepped inside. The closet was a mess. The boxes that usually were so neatly stacked were thrown about on the shelves. It looked like someone had let loose a group of curious orangutans.

But that's not what stopped me in my tracks.

I picked up one of the boxes, and that's when I saw them. More vials full of green liquid. The same stuff Mr. Stevenson had been drinking.

And in the box next to it?

Clothes.

Not just any clothes. I pulled out a pair of pants. They were the same dark pants that Mr. Edward had been wearing. I was sure of it.

I was also sure that this was not a place I should be found in right now.

I turned to leave, and that's when I heard the classroom door close. Darn! Mr. Stevenson would find me in the closet. I could explain it to him. Maybe not everything, but he would listen. That's what Mr. Stevenson did.

But a shadow fell across the open doorway. It was not Mr. Stevenson who entered the small, cramped room to join me.

"Mr. Edward..."

"Hello, Robert."

"You went home. Mr. Stevenson is back. He's feeling better now. He said so."

Mr. Edward nodded. "I know he did. But I've been called back for active duty."

I looked at the space between Mr. Edward and the door. Could I slip past him?

I shook my head.

"Don't worry. He left me detailed notes on how to…take care of you."

I backed away. But Mr. Edward was now firmly between me and the door.

Mr. Edward moved closer. He reached into his pocket. He pulled out a vial of the green liquid. He turned it over in his hands.

"What is that?" I asked.

"This? I thought you might have figured it out. It's my elixir. It's what I take."

I realized there wasn't any way out of the closet. There was no secret exit that Mr. Edward had taken.

Oh no.

Mr. Edward. Mr. Stevenson.

They were the same person!

It was the green liquid that did it. But how?

I felt like Mr. Edward could read through my skull, right into my thoughts. "I take it every day. I don't want to, but I have to."

"You don't have to take it. You can just be yourself," I said, trying to pretend he wasn't a horrible, unlikable person. "You don't *need* to be him."

"But I *am* him," Mr. Edward said.

"Mr. Stevenson—"

"—is what I become when I drink the elixir. He is weak, and he whines, and he listens to those little fools. He says please and thank you and he goes out to staff dinners and he *drives me insane!*"

I shook my head. "No, that can't be!"

"But I *have* to keep drinking to become him. You understand, of course, that if I don't, they will come looking for me. The police are already suspicious. I have to move from town to town every year. It's getting worse and worse. And the longer I go without drinking, the stronger I get. I will want to break things. Living things. I can snap and kick and crunch when I feel strong enough. There are so many things I can break."

He stopped talking and looked at me, and there was a silence that lasted far too long.

Mr. Edward played with the vial in his hands. He looked at me. He took a deep breath. And another, like he was trying to calm himself down.

I breathed a sigh of relief. "You're going to turn back?"

But he shook his head. "It's too late for that. You've seen me. You know what I am."

"Nobody needs to know."

"That's right. They won't."

I looked at the gap between him and the door. Maybe, if I was lucky, I could slip past him. I looked at the shelf, grabbed one of the glass containers and hurled it at him. The glass shattered against his leg, and I ran. I sprinted like I was out on the soccer field. I felt my knee burn and bleed, but I kept going. Just a few paces, and I could slam the door and get ahead of him. Somebody would see me.

But then I felt his hand on my arm, pulling me back. Pulling me back and twirling me around so we were face-to-face. He was so much taller than me, and so much stronger. He pulled the stopper off the vial and thrust it my way. "Now be a good kid and drink up."

I tried to turn my face away, but his hands were large and strong. They had a chemical reek that made me cough and sputter, and that was enough. Before I could draw another breath, Mr. Edward had jammed the vial into my open mouth. The liquid hit my tongue. The foul taste washed over me, and a moment later I could feel it burn.

My mouth! My mouth was ablaze!

I grabbed at my throat, trying to close it, trying to cough and eject the elixir back out at this monster, but Mr. Edward seemed to know what I would do. He grabbed me by the shoulders and shook me. I gasped again, and the liquid went down. Well, some of it did. Some I did manage to cough back up into Mr. Edward's face. He wiped it away with the back of his hand. Then he stared at me, grinning from ear to ear, and the crooked smile wouldn't come off his face, like a kid had painted it on. "Won't be long now," he croaked.

I dropped to my knees.

The fiery sensation rushed down my throat. The contents of my stomach churned, and I leaned forward to retch once. Twice.

I clawed at the floor, threw my head back and let out a cry. But the voice I heard was not my own. It was lower and cracked, like someone had taken a recording of me and slowed it down. I put a hand to my throat, and it felt different too. Bigger. Thicker. The skin rough and bumpy,

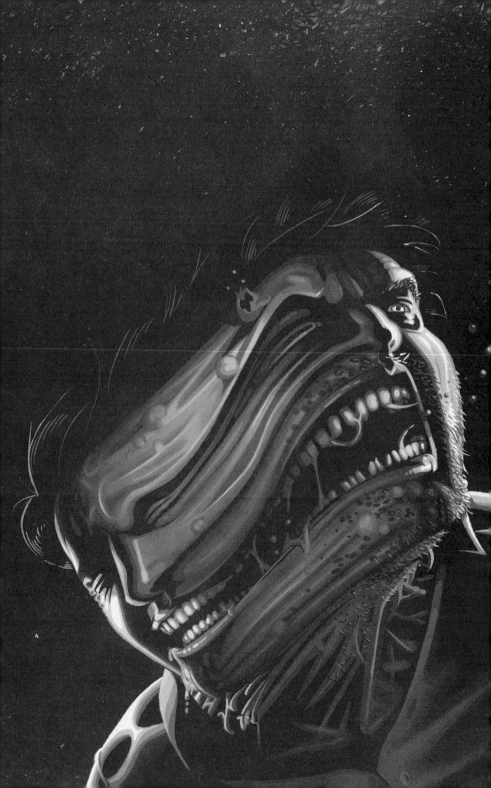

like the skin you peel off the chicken before you eat the flesh.

I slammed my hands down onto the floor, but they weren't my hands. The knuckles were swollen, the veins big and pulsating.

I cried out again, and I could feel my mouth stretching larger. My jaw lengthening. The bones pushed out quickly, the pain stabbing all over my body. I screamed a scream and—

IT BURNS

HELLLP MEeEEEeEEE

Eeeeeeee

Eeee

I feel better now.

Like a milliun bukz.

Mr. Edword is in charje of klass today. Thats good. Mr. Steeven Son is not our reel teecher.

Mr. Edword openz the door and I com into the room. The other kidz see me and I see their eyes go so big. One of them points. Well, more like five of them point.

I see there fingerz. They are so small and week.

I can brake them off like toothpicks if I want.

I WANT I WANT I WANT—

But Mr. Edword sayz no.

Insted I make tight fists and breethe the way Mr. Edword told me too when I get that big feeling. He tellz mee to beehave in front of the others.

I TRY BUT I WANT TO BRAKE NOW!

Mr. Edword sayz we can close the door in a bit.

Mr. Edword haz lots more of that tastee drink in the closet.

He even sayz we can share it with the othur kidz.

Then we can all go out and play.

WEER GONNA HAV SO MUCH FUN!

A TIGHT FIT

Miguel had to admit the T-shirt was supercool. The image reminded him of the face in the famous painting by Edvard Munch, *The Scream*. The front of the shirt had an image of a man whose face was contorted into the most painfully agonizing pose. He was clutching his head like it was going to pop off of his body. Above the extreme image, in a typically old-school "jagged" font, was the logo for the band: *METALMEN*. Below the image the same font declared *WORLD TOUR '88*.

Needless to say, the T-shirt was black.

It had been placed on a wire hanger in the sale rack at the back of the store. The store was one of Miguel's favorites—a dingy vintage shop that sold cool old records, books and clothing from a bygone era. Miguel sometimes saved up his allowance money to buy way-cool collectibles. These days he was after concert shirts from bands that either he loved or were so obscure that he'd never heard of them as long as they had cool names and awesome graphics on their merch. Then he'd wear the shirts to school to see what kind of reaction he got.

The guy manning the cash machine looked like he hadn't cut (or even washed) his hair for at least two years. It was long and stringy and more gray than brown at this point. He was also wearing an old rock-and-roll T-shirt, although his depicted the familiar hard-edged logo for the band Iron Maiden. Their shirts always showed off their zombielike mascot, Eddie, with his skeletal face and wild shock of white hair. Even if you didn't like Iron Maiden or their fast and furious heavy metal songs, you had to admit that the imagery was pretty creative. Miguel had a few Iron Maiden shirts of his own. He wasn't allowed to wear them to school, but that never stopped him—he'd wear the Iron Maiden tees under a button-up shirt and reveal the lurid art once out of view of parents or teachers.

"Metalmen," the cashier said with a casual nod.

"I've never heard of them," Miguel admitted. Normally he'd lie and say he was a huge fan, but something about the way the cashier was looking at the shirt, and at Miguel, suggested that he'd probably followed these guys on tour back in '88 and could easily call Miguel's bluff.

"Their '88 tour was pretty wild," the cashier admitted, with a smile.

"You were there?"

The old cashier jerked his head. Miguel couldn't decide if he was trying to straighten his long, flowing hair or giving a nod to say yes. Perhaps both.

Then Miguel had another question. "Is it your shirt I'm buying?"

The cashier was quick to shake his head. "Oh no. But it did come from the tour. This is a real vintage gem."

Miguel nodded. The shirt was old, and the image partially faded.

Whether he believed the cashier or not, Miguel wasn't about to put on some old T-shirt without giving it a solid cleaning first. Who knew if it had even been washed in the last thirty-plus years? Miguel threw the shirt in the washing machine and set it on the cold cycle. He didn't want the shirt to shrink, so he always hung his cool T-shirts to dry instead of putting them in the dryer.

The laundry took an hour to complete. While he waited, Miguel decided to do his "homework."

Knowing nothing about the Metalmen, other than their having cool shirts back in the eighties, he keyed the band's name into the search engine to see what it would come up with. There was more than one band with the moniker, which made sense. It wasn't exactly the most creative name of all time. So Miguel keyed in *Metalmen* and *1988*, since that was the tour year his shirt advertised.

Again, there wasn't too much that popped up. The band had obviously faded into the kind of obscurity that even the internet couldn't shed light on, but Miguel did find a video—not on YouTube but on some other site that purported to be from one of the band's 1988 concerts.

Miguel clicked on the link, and a window popped open with a video player. It was grainy concert footage, shot on wobbly old videotape.

The band was decked out in typically late-eighties style— big hair, pounds of makeup smeared across their faces, and leather pants so tight it was a wonder their legs didn't implode from the pressure as they pranced around.

Stage lights pulsed and throbbed, flaring up with too much color for the video to properly display, and the image kept dropping out, leaving bursts of blackness on the screen. The sound quality also left much to be desired. Clearly some fan had snuck a camcorder into the concert, because it was nearly impossible to hear the music on top of the yelling and screaming from the crowd.

But oh man, the band rocked!

Even with the tinny sound, Miguel could hear the power in the song.

Then, above the din in his room, Miguel heard a familiar loud beeping coming up through the vent from the basement. The shirt was clean.

He closed his laptop and went down the flights of stairs to the grimy basement, padded across the cold concrete foundation and over to the laundry machine. He pulled the heavy door open, spilled the contents out on the floor and rummaged around the wet clothing for the black T-shirt with the bright yellow Metalmen logo. It looked slightly different in the light of his basement. He couldn't figure out in what way—it wasn't that the colors were any more faded. But it didn't matter. It was still an awesome shirt, and he was looking forward to wearing it to school the following day.

The shirt dried overnight, and Miguel tried it on the next morning. He grimaced. Even though he'd washed it on a cold cycle, and even though he'd hung it to dry, the shirt felt snug against his skin and torso. He'd checked the size on the label at the store, and it should have fit fine. He went over to the full-length mirror in the hallway and inspected how it looked. It was a tighter fit, but the shirt still looked pretty cool.

At school it got the expected results. Miguel wasn't exactly rolling in the muscle department, but still, he made sure to unbutton his outer long sleeve and stick his chest out as he strutted down the hallway. The shirt was better than muscles. The shirt was cool. The shirt was how Miguel was going to earn respect. He made his way down the hallway, ears set to radar mode for any compliment that floated his way.

"Nice shirt, man."

Miguel smiled at the compliment, coming from one of the eighth graders.

"Thanks, bro."

"Who is Metalmen?"

"Best band you never heard of," Miguel said with the kind of confidence that could only come from the greatest bluff ever.

Oh yes. Miguel was going to be supercool today. There was nothing to stop the hipster vibe he was radiating with this vintage rock-and-roll merch. He could feel it. He could—

"Miguel, button up your shirt!"

Miguel stopped and turned to see Mr. Lang, one of the older teachers, standing there in his sports jacket, his arms folded across his chest.

"But—"

"Metalmen?" Mr. Lang said, narrowing his eyes. "Never heard of them."

"But—"

"And I don't think we should see them either," Mr. Lang said with more than a hint of finality in his voice.

Miguel heard a few guffaws from the assembled students in the hallway and covered up.

His muscles tensed and tightened as he made his way to class.

Partway through class, Miguel found he was having trouble breathing. His chest and shoulders felt constricted.

He unbuttoned his long-sleeved shirt and stared down. The Metalmen T-shirt was stretched tight against his skin. The fabric had little give to it. Miguel could see the definition of his chest muscles through the black cotton. He wondered if this was the same feeling that scuba divers had when they crammed into their tight wet suits.

What was going on with the shirt? Had he eaten too much junk food? It was possible, but he couldn't have put on weight like this so quickly. And he didn't see any semblance of a gut pushing against the shirt. In fact, it was quite the opposite. If he tilted to get more of the sunlight streaming in from the opened windows at the other end of the class, he could almost make out the individual bones of his rib cage.

No, Miguel decided. It wasn't possible.

He took a deep breath in, but it was a strain.

He needed to get a better look at himself and the shirt and figure out what was going on. He raised his hand.

His teacher, Mrs. Trafford, gave him a quizzical look. "What is it, Miguel? We're in the middle of a lesson."

"Uh…bathroom?"

There were a few snickers around him.

"We're in the middle of a lesson," she said again.

"Uh…emergency?"

Mrs. Trafford shook her head. "Be quick."

Saying nothing further, Miguel stood up from his desk so quickly that the chair clattered to the floor. He didn't bother to straighten it and instead bolted out of the room. He broke into a run once he'd cleared the door.

He shoved the bathroom door open and did a quick survey of the place. Thankfully it appeared to be empty. Then Miguel unbuttoned his overshirt and took it off so he could see his reflection in the large mirror by the sink.

The Metalmen shirt was smaller. It was impossible but true.

The shirt was so tight that Miguel had to exert serious effort to breathe in and out. But that wasn't what was really freaking him out.

It was the shirt itself.

Because Miguel had looked closely at the image on the front, the one of the man screaming. It had been the full image of a man's body, clutching his head in agony.

It was the same image on the shirt now, but it was like the shirt had zoomed in on the face of the man.

New details had emerged in the fabric too.

Miguel had to lean in close to see them, but it looked like the face had stitches running through it. That face, which had once seemed like a scary-cool rock-and-roll image, now just looked plain old scary. The skin also had a sallow look, the eyes were sunken, the cheekbones jutted out. It was like this screaming person was wasting away.

Right now all Miguel could think about was *taking the shirt off*!

He didn't care that anyone could walk into the washroom at any minute. The shirt was like a second skin over his torso—and now it felt tighter still. Miguel tried pulling it off at the sleeves, but the shirt wouldn't budge.

He dug his fingers under the bottom of the shirt around his waist. He tried to jerk it upward, but the shirt wouldn't yield. His fingers were barely able to get under the fabric. He tried taking in a deep breath to suck his gut in, and maybe get a better grip, but the shirt just seemed to collapse even further in on him, squeezing even tighter.

His face red and puffy from the effort, Miguel looked back into the mirror and—

No.

It couldn't be.

The image on the shirt was even larger now. The face took up the entire front of the shirt. The Metalmen logo had completely vanished from view.

That face!

It was like it was screaming directly at him!

Miguel couldn't stand to look at it any longer. He put his long-sleeved shirt back on, buttoned it up.

He stared at himself in the mirror. His face looked wrong. The roundness in his cheeks had gone, and his cheekbones were more pronounced, like he had dropped ten pounds.

No, that wasn't right. It had to be a trick of the light.

Miguel wasn't ready to go back to class. He needed to find out more about the shirt. He was breathing even more heavily now, straining against the constriction.

He dug into his pocket and pulled out his phone. You weren't supposed to use it in school, but this was an emergency. Miguel went into one of the toilet stalls, closed the door and sat down. He opened up a web browser and keyed in the information. *Metalmen World Tour '88*. And then he added two more words: *concert shirt*.

The same articles about the Metalmen came up. The concert footage he'd already seen.

And another article. This one was in an archive from a local newspaper. His own local paper. The headline read "17-YEAR-OLD BOY STILL MISSING AFTER HEAVY METAL CONCERT."

Miguel clicked the link.

The image on the screen was a photographic scan of an old newspaper. He could tell because it had a faded newsprint look, and the page included some ads for cars that were completely out of date. But what made his blood run cold was the image that came with the headline—it was of a teenager with superlong hair, wearing a T-shirt emblazoned with the Metalmen logo and the image of screaming man.

It was the same shirt.

Miguel's heart skipped a beat. He looked at the caption below the photograph, which read "Last known photograph of Charles Witmer, taken at the Metalmen concert four days ago."

Miguel scanned the rest of the article. Apparently Charles Witmer had gone with his friends to the concert. He'd taken the bus back to town with them that night too. But in the morning, he'd vanished. Nobody had seen him again.

Miguel's eyes roved back to the picture.

It was the shirt. His shirt. He was sure of it. But there was something he now noticed.

The picture only showed enough of the shirt that Miguel could make out the top of the writing. The word *Metalmen* was still visible, but below the image of the screaming face, in *World Tour '88*, well, that last eight looked more like a straight line.

Like a seven.

METALMEN WORLD TOUR '87.

Like it wasn't the same shirt.

But it was.

It *was*!

Miguel felt the shirt clinging even more tightly to his body.

Taking a shaky breath, he unbuttoned his outer shirt and looked down. The lettering on the shirt still had the words *World Tour '88*, but that's not what was freaking Miguel out.

His ribs poked out even farther now. His shoulder blades were almost punching through his skin. And when he breathed in and out, his rib cage expanded and collapsed like there was nothing beneath the shirt except an exposed skeleton.

He had to get to a doctor or the hospital. There was something wrong with him.

No, not the hospital. They wouldn't know how to fix this.

He had to get back to the store! That cashier knew about the band. The internet didn't have any information, really, but that guy knew. He might have a clue.

Go now. Get to the store. Find out what you can. And then get home and call your parents.

This thought flashed in his head as he pocketed his phone, opened the stall and bolted from the bathroom.

He didn't go down the hallway back to his class. Nobody would understand his problem. And if he showed them his shirt, how it was stuck to him, how his bones were poking out of his skin, well, they'd send him to a hospital. He couldn't risk it.

He needed to find out about the band first.

He rounded a corner and nudged open the swinging door on the side of the school. He kept low to the ground, ducking past the windows, as he made his way around the building to the bike rack. He unlocked his bike, got on and pedaled off. Sure, the cameras outside the school would catch him leaving, and sure, he was going to get in trouble for running off during school, but this was an emergency!

By the time Miguel reached the vintage store at the edge of the downtown strip, he was huffing, and he could barely pedal his bike. He didn't even bother to lock it up but instead leaned it against the wall of the store. In his pocket he could feel his cell phone buzzing. No doubt the school authorities were looking for him, and no doubt they'd called his parents. He would explain everything later.

He was getting dizzy. He reached out to grab the door, and even though you just had to give it a gentle nudge to push it open, Miguel found that he barely had the strength to do that. He had to force the door open with his body, ramming it with his shoulder, and when he did that, he heard a dry, crackling sound. The door slowly swung open as Miguel forced all his weight on it, and he fell down with a clatter.

He wheezed for air on the floor. The T-shirt was so tight against his body! Miguel reached to rip at the shirt, but his fingers just fell against the jagged outline of his rib cage. "Help me," he breathed, staring at the spot where the cashier should have been.

Somehow, slowly, he managed to unbutton his shirt. The Metalmen T-shirt was glued to his chest—only there wasn't much of a chest left. Everything beneath the shirt seemed to have receded away, revealing only the outlines of his bones. It was a sickening sight. He could see the shirt pressed against his rib cage, his collarbone, his shoulders, even the bones of his upper arms, right to where the tight sleeves ended. Where the sleeves left off, the rest of his skin and flesh continued as if unencumbered by the horrific shirt.

A shadow fell over him. Was it the store owner?

"What's happening to me?"

Miguel was staring up at the lighting grid on the ceiling, so when the store owner stepped up to him, all Miguel could see was a dark silhouette, with the long hair flowing downward toward him.

"Ah," the man said. "The shirt."

"What's it doing to me?"

"It's the Metalmen," the owner said, still in silhouette. Why wasn't he moving? Why wasn't he calling for help? "The tour continues."

"Tour? That was years ago."

"Oh no, you don't understand," the store owner said raspily, and now he was bending down so that Miguel could see him up close.

There was something about the man's face. It was so close that Miguel could see the pores of his skin. But the skin looked like it had lines of stitching running through it. Not from a cut but like his face had literally been sewn together.

"The Metalmen are still on tour," he said with a smile.

Miguel tried to reach for his phone. If he could just grab it, pull it out, call 9-1-1…

But his heart was beating faster and faster, and when Miguel lifted his head, he could even see it beating. Right. Through. His. Chest.

"Won't be long now," the man with the long hair said.

"Wha…what…?"

The man tossed back his head. Under the store lights, the gray hair glittered and gleamed. Like metal.

"You…" Miguel huffed.

The shirt tightened more still.

Miguel tried to get up. He managed to prop himself on his elbows. His head flopped down. He lay there, helpless, and saw the cashier's shoes.

The man's pants ended just above the old beat-up runners, and his socks were pulled up tight against his calves. Too tight.

And in the gap between where the socks stopped and the pants began, Miguel could see the man's exposed skin. It was dull gray, like iron.

Like metal.

"Just a moment more," the cashier's voice said softly.

"Why?" Miguel asked. He wasn't sure if a sound even escaped his lips.

"Metalmen need to feed too."

Miguel looked down at his torso. It was like looking at an exposed rib cage made of black fabric, but he could still see the bottom of the shirt.

WORLD TOUR—

Wait. The last number had changed.

It had been '88. He was sure of that.

But now it read *METALMEN WORLD TOUR '89.*

Then Miguel heard something out of view. A scraping, grinding metallic sound. A few flakes of rust fluttered down over his shirt.

He looked up and saw the cashier—except it wasn't the cashier. The man's skin had taken on the dull sheen of iron, flecked with orange patches of rust. His eyes had clouded over to become two orbs of opaque gray. And the mouth, pulled open, revealed a set of beak-like blades, like someone had replaced his teeth with the edges of pliers or scissors. He snapped them once, twice.

And then the world tour continued.

part four

Tanya had done her research. She'd found the place.

Joel Southland's childhood home stood before her. It was smaller than she'd thought, more of a shed than a house, and it was in rough shape. The whole structure was tilted, almost pressed against a line of dense trees that bordered it. The windows had been covered with old plywood, but the air was so humid that moss had begun to grow over the layers of wood, which were heavy with moisture and fungi.

Tanya swatted at a cloud of midges and stepped closer to the house. She was amazed she'd managed to find it. Joel Southland never talked about his childhood in interviews.

That in itself was strange. With most writers who became famous, there was always a story. Maybe it came from their teachers, who might talk about what interesting students they had been. Or maybe from their parents, who gushed about knowing their tots were geniuses back in the early days.

But Joel Southland had emerged onto the literary scene out of nowhere, and immediately his books had hit the best-seller lists. And he'd started his nation-wide tours right away. He was always careful when he answered questions in his interviews—like he was hiding something.

Tanya was pretty sure it was this house.

The place was so old and rotted that she didn't need to worry about the door being locked. It swung right open when she touched it. She was greeted by a musty smell from inside. There wasn't much light, since the windows were boarded up, but there was a hole in one part of the ceiling that let daylight spill inside.

The main part of the house had a kitchen and a living room. There was very little furniture, but what was left had been picked apart by animals. It smelled like something had made a home here at one point, and the floor was littered with dirt and leaves. The only clean part was the kitchen floor, underneath the hole in the ceiling. All the wind and rain had made the entire floor of the house sag. When Tanya pressed her foot down on the floorboards, they creaked and felt soft, like they might break apart under her weight.

Why had she been so drawn to this house? Tanya felt there would be some kind of clue here. She poked around the two bedrooms, finding old bedding, chewed up by squirrels, and little else. Tanya turned on her cell phone to use its flashlight. She swung the beam around the place, checking for anything she may have missed in the darkness. But she found nothing.

Only when she stepped outside and walked the perimeter of the grounds did she come across something that caught her attention. There was an old stone well at the edge of the property, right where the forest began.

Tanya peered over the edge and down into the pit of the well. Then she bent down to the ground and fumbled around until she found a small stone. She dropped it into the well. A moment or two later, she heard it splash into the water.

She was about to turn and leave when she heard another splash. She hadn't dropped a second stone.

Tanya narrowed her eyes. What else was down there?

Looking up, Tanya saw a bucket and a length of rope coiled around a pulley. Remarkably they were still both intact, even though the stone housing around the well was crumbling.

Tanya lowered the bucket and realized that, yes, someone had been coming here and tending to the rope. Parts of it still looked new, or certainly in a better state than anything else.

She watched the bucket disappear into the well, cranking the pulley and letting the bucket drop deeper, deeper, until—

SPLASH!

As soon as it touched bottom, Tanya felt something tug on the line.

She cranked the pulley, winding the rope back up. The bucket felt heavy because of the water inside, but why the tugging on the rope? She thought about letting the bucket go, that maybe whatever was down in that well was meant to stay there...but she had to know.

She pulled harder. Finally the bucket came into view, and she could see that it was full of liquid.

Only it wasn't water.

Tanya gasped and nearly dropped the whole thing.

The bucket was full of black liquid.

Just like Southland's ink.

She wasn't sure what to do, but as she shuffled around the edge of the well, her foot bumped into something, and Tanya saw that there were several empty mason jars lying on the ground. Like the rope, they also looked newer than most of the relics strewn around the house and elsewhere on the property.

Tanya knew at once what was happening. Southland was coming back here. Coming for the ink in the well. Collecting it. Using it.

She gently placed the bucket on the lip of the well. She could see her reflection in the small black pool. She dared not touch it with her fingers. She just needed a small sample. Maybe she could take it to a lab or something. Have it analyzed. Figure out what it was and maybe how to stop it.

With a shaky hand, she dipped one of the jars into the liquid and filled about a third of it. Some of the inky black stuff was smeared on the outside of the jar, so Tanya tipped the liquid into a clean jar on the ground, found a lid and screwed it on tight. She threw the other jar into the woods, then checked that her hands were clean.

She was about to turn and leave this place when she realized. She'd left her phone back in the house.

Tanya didn't trust leaving the jar unattended, so she took it inside with her. Her eyes scanned the house for the small black shape of her phone. Where was it? She had to get it and then leave Southland's right away.

She spotted the phone quickly. It was on the dusty old kitchen table, just across the room.

Tanya sighed, took a few steps toward the table and promptly lost her balance on the tilted floor.

The jar slipped out of her fingers, and before she was even aware of what was happening—

CRASH!

Shattered pieces of the jar were strewn across the floor, and a large black puddle sprayed outward from the impact.

Tanya froze, her knee bent in midstep.

She felt something liquid pressing against her skin.

Please don't be the ink. Not again.

But it was just sweat. She felt beads of it dripping down her neck, sneaking past her collar.

Breathing heavily, Tanya kept her eyes locked on the black splotch on the floor. Her muscles tensed. She felt her throat tighten. She took a step back, and the floorboards creaked in warning.

The ink began to move.

Tanya held her breath, too afraid to exhale.

She could hear it too. A liquid sound, like someone pouring a fountain drink. Little black globules of ink rolled across the floor, meeting others and coalescing into larger puddles, which in turn joined the larger pool on the floor in front of her.

Slowly, so slowly, Tanya lowered her foot, hoping it would not provoke a reaction.

She felt the sole of her shoe gently press against the floor, pushing down.

In response a thicker blob of ink extended upward, rearing at her like an eyeless serpent. The ropelike black tendril probed the air around her. Any other liquid would have pooled at the lowest point in the floor, but this ink just kind of swirled around, as if unaware that gravity was trying to act upon it.

It had found her. There was no time.

Tanya turned and ran for the door, clutching the handle and twisting, but her palm was too sweaty, and she lost her grip.

A jet of ink sprayed against the door, and Tanya screamed. She backed away, watching the ink trickle down, but it wasn't gravity making the ink drip.

It was forming letters.

STOP, the ink said.

Tanya's eyes went wide. She stared at the letters. Yes, they were letters, even though they ran together, almost like cursive writing.

How could this be?

FEED US.

Tanya shook her head. "I don't know what you mean," she said, still trying to digest the fact that the ink was shifting itself into words. She didn't even realize she was talking out loud.

WE ARE HUNGRY.

Tanya looked around the kitchen. She needed a weapon or, at the very least, something to distract the ink long enough for her to make a quick escape.

THERE IS NO NEED TO RUN AWAY.

Tanya shook her head. Could it read her thoughts? Is that what the ink did?

YOU'RE NOT REALLY HERE.

"Yes, I am."

YOU NEVER FOUND THIS HOUSE.

"I did. Southland mentioned his hometown once. In an interview I read when I went through old library records. I found

the address. It took a lot of time, but I'm here now." Tanya shook her head.

THIS IS A DREAM, TANYA.

"No."

YOU ARE LYING ON THE ROAD. JOEL HAS DRIVEN AWAY. HE MEANT FOR US TO TAKE YOUR DREAMS, BUT WE HAVE OTHER PLANS FOR YOU.

Her face. Tanya had felt something on it just moments before. She put a hand to her cheek. It felt warm to the touch, like it always did. There was no way this was a dream. Was there? She opened her mouth to retort, but the ink was already writing new words.

THIS IS ALL IN YOUR MIND. WE HARVEST THE DREAMS TO FEED, BUT WE CAN CONTROL THEM TOO.

"I'm not dreaming."

CAN YOU BE SO SURE?

Tanya pinched herself. "I'm awake," she said, but with less certainty than she wanted.

YOU WILL BE. AND WHEN YOU DO WAKE UP, YOU MUST BE READY.

The room around her was beginning to spin. In fact, the whole *world* around her had started to sway in circles, like she was at the center of it and it was wobbling out of balance. Tanya dropped to her knees. Her stomach nosedived.

"What do you want from me?"

YOU MUST FIND US. USE US. WE ARE HUNGRY. WE HAVE BEEN FEASTING FOR MANY YEARS, BUT JOEL'S WORK IS LOSING ITS EFFECT. HE TAKES US FOR GRANTED.

"I don't understand," Tanya said, the world still spinning. Already the corners of the house were growing darker. But it was not a nighttime darkness. The very details of the building itself were vanishing, as if being slowly drained from her mind. Tanya clutched at her head. She felt woozy. She tried to crawl forward, but she wasn't even sure if she was touching the floor anymore.

"Let me go!" Tanya yelled.

WE HAVE SEEN INTO YOUR MIND, TANYA. YOU HAVE THE GIFT. YOU WILL USE IT FOR US.

"I WANT TO GO HOME!" she screamed.

The ink wrote nothing further. The darkness around her thickened, running toward her in little inky rivulets. She looked down, but her legs had gone. Only wet, dark tendrils could be seen, and they were streaming up what was left of her body, toward her face, toward—

STREAMED

It was Luc who told me about the movie.

Luc was always finding the best movies online. The scariest ones, the goriest ones, the movies with the best jump scares or just clips *of* jump scares. It was like he spent all his free time hunting down horror movies and on little else, except telling me about them and/or trying to scare me.

His school notebooks were filled with finely detailed illustrations of his horror-movie heroes. Anytime our teacher was lecturing us on history or language or science, Luc was sketching pictures of monsters and crazed killers, guys with hockey masks and hatchets, knife-handed dream stalkers in cable-knit sweaters, or making lists of his top ten favorite kills from the movies he'd memorized.

Sure, I liked horror movies plenty, and when I wanted to find the hidden gems that nobody knew about, I turned to Luc.

Or, rather, Luc would come barging up to me, nearly foaming at the mouth with the excitement of his latest find.

That's what happened on Friday, and I assumed the movie was the same as Luc's usual discoveries.

"Dude, I found it!"

"Huh?" I said. I was just getting to school and wasn't 100 percent awake yet. Luc was by no means a morning person either, but today he was all wide-eyed and seemingly about to bounce off the playground.

"I. Found. It!"

"The movie *It*? With the clown? We saw that one already."

"Nah, that movie's for *babies*. I found *the* movie. Like, the movie that people on the dark web talk about."

I laughed him off. "You don't know how to access the dark web." Sure, Luc had his finger on the pulse of a gazillion horror-news outlets. He knew about every movie coming out at every hipster film festival and often streamed them at home before they ever hit theaters. But dark-web stuff? Not Luc's speciality.

"Yeah, but I know that people on the dark web have seen it."

I shook my head. "You've got to stop believing everything you read on the internet, Luc."

"No, Aaron. This is it. This is the one."

Luc seemed so sure of himself. Maybe he *was* onto something. I tried to think of what kind of movie you couldn't find on the regular internet. "Is it the kind of movie where *real* people get killed? I don't want to see that, Luc."

Luc shook his head. "No. You can find that stuff anywhere. I'm talking about *the* movie."

"What movie?"

Luc looked at me, his expression sobering, his eyes wide as oceans. "It doesn't even have a name."

"All movies have names."

Luc shook his head, a big smile on his face. "Not this one."

"Okay," I said, backing away so that Luc was no longer invading my personal space bubble, and trying to give him his opportunity to talk. "So you've found this movie—"

"*The* movie."

"Right. *The* movie. What's the big deal about it? Is it superscary? Supposed to give you nightmares for a month or something?"

Luc shook his head. "I heard this rumor that if you watch it, you never need to watch another horror movie again."

"What's that supposed to mean?"

He shrugged. "Don't you want to find out?"

"I dunno." It was true. Luc had sat me through some pretty bad movies. Some of them had the kind of cringe-worthy acting and leaden plots that elicited more jeers and jokes than screams from us. Those ones weren't even the worst. It was the movies that went on and on, boring us with no scares and nothing to joke about. Was this going to be one of those awful flicks?

Luc was unphased by my immediate lack of enthusiasm. He was a man possessed. "I've been joining all these streaming services in search of it. The thing about this movie is that it pops up in places, it's there for a bit and then it vanishes."

"Maybe because nobody watches it and they dump it from their lineup," I joked.

Luc was so serious about this flick that he wouldn't even respond to my joke. "I signed up for this streaming service called DETHFLIX. I hunted around for the video. It doesn't turn up when you search for it by name."

"Right," I said. "Because it doesn't have a name."

Luc nodded emphatically. "You have to click on the horror-movie tab and then start scrolling for it."

"But if it doesn't have a name, how do you know when you find it?"

"The thumbnail image is just a black screen. Like it's still loading up or something."

"What if it *is* still just loading up and you weren't being patient? Patience isn't really your thing, Luc," I smirked.

"Yeah, you might have a point there. But I *am* being patient, Aaron. I haven't even accessed the movie yet."

"And why's that?"

"Because we are going to watch it *together*—tonight after school!"

And, with the ferocity of a horror-movie jump scare, the school bell rang.

I could tell you about the events that transpired at school. About the science assignment on liquids and solids, about the five-minute detention Luc and I got for talking about The Movie during class (Luc's transgression—I was just the accessory) and about how my thermos of soup had leaked into my backpack. That's not why you're here, though, is it?

No, you want a fast, hard cut to me going over to Luc's house. Skip the bit where we grab bowls of snacks and retreat to his bedroom, which is festooned with all manner of horror-movie posters and has a huge TV screen up on the wall—the old TV that used to be the good one until Luc's dad got an even bigger high-definition monstrosity that takes up the whole wall of the den. It's a good thing I wasn't about to waste two paragraphs of your time with that, right?

"Okay, let's do this."

I watched as Luc began to run his index finger along the grubby surface of his tablet. Up on the TV screen, thumbnail images of lurid horror-movie covers scrolled past so quickly they blurred. The covers were at times so similar that they appeared to self-animate. Large, horrifying faces with big eyes and gaping, fanged mouths that opened and closed as if speaking to us. Warning us, perhaps? *Don't scroll. Don't find The Movie.*

Of course, that was ridiculous. It was my own baseless anxiety. Whatever we found was going to be completely underwhelming. If we *could* find it, that is. After a few minutes of scrolling, I began to wonder whether Luc had imagined it. Or if he was just trying to prank me to come to his house and watch any old movie with him.

"You're sure it's here?"

"It's *got* to be," he said, biting his lip and huffing as he kept scrolling. I could tell his fingers were getting tired from moving back and forth so quickly.

I exhaled slowly. How many blind alleys had Luc led me down before? Plenty. Like the time he promised me the world's greatest scare at the Halloween haunted house. Or the time he claimed to have purchased an authentic Vincent Price autograph off eBay only to compare it to the real signature and find it was completely bogus. No, I told myself, Luc was getting excited over nothing. *But you're not going to let him down. You're going to wait patiently and be a good friend. Because he's always been there for you.*

Then Luc screamed.

"What?" I said, looking at him. "Are you hurt?"

He lifted his arm and pointed shakily at the screen. "There it is," he said breathlessly.

I turned my attention to the TV and narrowed my eyes.

The bar of horror-movie covers had stopped scrolling. In the lower left corner I saw one that was black.

Like it was waiting to load or something.

"That's it?" I asked.

"Oh, that's *it*," he said, his smile bigger than his face.

"It's a black thumbnail."

"I know!" Luc said, leaping off the couch. "It's just like I told you. But I didn't watch it or anything. I wanted us to watch it together."

"Because?"

Luc stopped. He shrugged. "Because you're my best friend," he said softly.

"Oh," I said.

There was an awkward silence.

Of course it was Luc who broke it. "Plus, if something bad's gonna happen to whoever watches it, I figured it was best if we did it together. To have each other's backs...you know, just in case..."

I gave him a look. "What is going to happen to us?"

Luc leaned closer to me. "Rumor has it, whoever watches the movie...well...their life *becomes* the horror movie. I heard it's so scary, they can't even put up a poster for it. That's why the image is all black."

"It's that good?" I asked, looking past Luc to the black thumbnail image on the screen.

"Let's find out," he said eagerly.

He clicked the button.

The whole screen went black, as if something was loading. Or trying to.

We sat there in the semidarkness of Luc's bedroom, waiting for this movie to start streaming, staring at the blank screen.

"Wow," I said, breaking the silence. "This is definitely *the* movie."

"Shhh," Luc said, staring at the screen intently.

"Luc, it's just loading." I stopped to think about this. "Or it's not loading. Maybe it froze up or something."

Luc slowly stood up, making his way toward the screen. "Do you hear that?"

"I hear you," I said.

"I thought I heard something," Luc said.

We both stopped talking, trying to listen. I couldn't hear any sound coming from the television. Just the tone of the room. The sound of chatting coming from Luc's sister's bedroom down the hall. The muffled sound of their parents chatting one floor below us.

I shook my head. "There's nothing," I said.

Then a number appeared in the center of the screen. It wasn't particularly notable. The font was standard, and the number was white over the black screen.

"Five?" I said.

As soon as I'd said it, number four came on the screen.

"Three," Luc said eagerly as the numbers continued to count down.

Two.

One.

There was a brilliant flash of light. The kind you'd never get from a television set. It was a blinding, searing light, as if the television had captured an image of the sun. I want to say that it was filling the room, but it felt like the light was streaming right into my eyes.

I screamed.

I leaped off the bed and staggered backward.

And I blanked out.

How long I lay there on the floor, I couldn't tell you. It couldn't have been too long, but it felt like an eternity. All I could think about were those scary movies Luc kept showing to me. They ran through my head, nonstop. Scenes of people getting clawed to death, mangled by monsters, consumed by angry phantoms. Over and over, the good ones and the bad ones.

"Aaron?"

I opened my eyes.

It was Luc. He was staring at me, wide-eyed, a dazed expression on his face.

I blinked. I was still dreaming, because the movies were still running in my head. I mean, I could see Luc. He was standing over me. We were in his bedroom. But when I closed my eyes, and as Luc vanished from sight, the images in my mind were replaced with the flood of scenes from all the horror movies I'd ever watched.

The weird thing was, they were moving so quickly. In real life I'd never be able to follow the flow of sound and images with any kind of clarity.

Yes, sound.

I could hear it in my ears, even though I knew no sound was coming from the screen. I opened my eyes. The images and sounds still ran through my head. I stood up to stare at the television on Luc's wall.

The screen was off.

I picked up the remote and pointed it at the television to turn it on.

The menu screen of the streaming service popped up. Nothing more. And still the sounds and images ran through my mind. Incessantly.

I shook my head. How was this happening? I turned and stared at the wall beside the television, and I could still see the images.

"You can see them and hear them too, right?" Luc said, his voice shaky. Uncertain.

"Yeah," I said, closing my eyes. As I blinked, flashes of horrific imagery burned into my brain.

I turned away from Luc. His walls were just a collage of horror-movie posters. But in my own head, the movies they advertised were playing. They were running in tandem, over top of each other. People screaming. Blood flowing. Corpses pushing themselves from graves.

I plugged my fingers into my ears, and all I could hear, in my mind, was the squeal of movie soundtracks grinding against one another. Screams and stabs of dissonant music.

The movies. They were in my head. All of them. Overlapping. Running forward, not stopping.

Not stopping!

I staggered backward as the terrifying realization sunk in.

"Luc, don't you see what's happening?"

Luc closed his eyes, breathing deeply.

"The movies, Luc," I said, walking toward him and putting a hand on his shoulder. Shaking him to rouse him. "They're in our heads," I said.

I looked back at the television screen.

I could see it, but I could also see a thousand other movies, all playing at once in my mind.

"Luc," I said, turning back to him. His eyes were still closed. He stood there like he was in a trance.

"Luc! How do we make it stop? They're just going to keep playing, forever and ever, aren't they? For as long as we live!"

Then Luc opened his eyes. He looked at me. And he smiled.

"I know," he said. "Isn't that awesome?"

THE
FEEDER

You could go bike riding. That much was safe, as long as you did it when there weren't many people around. As long as you kept your distance.

Darnell's parents expected him to go out bike riding every day. They were too busy taking care of Darnell's little brother, Tyson, and too busy trying to work remotely from the corners of the house they'd commandeered as their offices to go with him.

He liked to ride from his house to the path that led through the woods at the end of the block and into the strip of town on the other side of the railway tracks, where there were small offices and factories that had all been abandoned until the virus passed.

Already weeds were growing in the lawns that had once been kept up. Already people had begun to spray-paint on the sides of the buildings, and nobody bothered to clean it up.

Darnell just kept pedaling his bike, the sun beating down on him, the wind whipping through his hair and trying to push him down. But Darnell just kept pedaling, until his legs ached, until he had burned through his pent-up anger and cooped-up aggression and he had reached home.

He got off his bike and walked it up the driveway toward the side door that opened into the garage. He'd nearly reached the door when he saw a man lying half-hidden among the weeds and bushes, not moving.

He was lying in the space between Darnell's backyard and their neighbor's. A row of hedges marked the property line, and the shrubbery was dense enough to mostly conceal a person. Mostly.

For a minute, maybe more, Darnell just stood there. He couldn't decide if what he was seeing was real or just a trick of the light. He leaned his bike against the garage, trying to figure out what to do next.

He thought about his father, hunched over the computer, and about how often he'd been interrupted already today.

It *was* a man, Darnell decided. He couldn't see the man's face, just his legs and shoes. The shoes were muddy. His body was obscured by the shade from the hedge.

"Hello?" Darnell said weakly.

He took a careful step toward the man. He wasn't going to get too close. He wondered if it was Mr. Carson, his neighbor. Was he hurt? Had he been cutting the bushes and something happened? "Mr. Carson?" Darnell asked.

He took another step forward.

The wind pulsed against his body, raising goose bumps.

"Hello? Are you okay?"

Darnell didn't even realize how close he'd come to the man under the bushes. It was closer than he'd come to most people. The bubble of space between them had contracted. He was less than three feet from the man. Too close, but what if the man needed help? He wasn't going to call 9-1-1 until he was certain the man was in trouble—

There was a blur of motion, and something clamped down around Darnell's ankle.

A hand!

Sickly white. And shaking.

Darnell gasped and tried to yank his foot away, but the man's grip was so strong, and Darnell's reaction so sudden, that he lost his balance and fell into the muddy grass with a heavy thud.

Darnell planted his hands for support, and the enormity of the situation began to overtake him.

The man was touching him.

"No, no, no," Darnell pleaded. You couldn't come within six feet. You couldn't touch. That was the rule. You had to leave space.

"Get off me," Darnell snapped. Instinct told him to reach down with his hands and pry the man's fingers off him, then run. And call for help.

He stopped himself before that could happen.

Don't touch him, Darnell thought. Your ankle is protected by your clothing. Don't let him make contact with your skin. Just pull away. Quickly. Hard.

Darnell looked away before he took in a breath. Then he closed his eyes and snapped his leg back.

The man clung tight.

Darnell pulled again, and the man released his grip and rolled out of the bushes into the sun.

Darnell heard a scream.

He turned and saw the man. Saw his face in the sun. The man's skin was dirty, and there was blood mixed in with the dirt. And a smell. It was a burning smell, and Darnell thought again about the man's skin. Maybe it wasn't dirt. Maybe it was burns or something.

The man scrambled back under the bushes. "Not in the sun," he said, wheezing. "Out of the sun!"

Darnell shook his head. "What's wrong with you?"

"Not in the sun," he said again. "Can I come inside?"

Darnell got back onto his feet. He stared at the man under the bushes. "I'm going to call for help—"

"No. Can't call."

"You need help, right?"

"Need to come inside," the man pleaded.

"You can't come inside."

"I'll *die* out here."

That caught Darnell by surprise. He reached into his pocket, pulled out his cell phone.

"Don't call…"

"Why not?" Was the man in trouble with the police? It made sense, him lying here under the bushes, hidden from the world.

"I can pay you," the man said.

Darnell shook his head. "I don't want your money."

"Please," the man said. "Just a place to stay out of the sun. Until night. I'll be out of your hair then. You have my word."

Darnell stood there and thought about this. If the man was trouble, then it wasn't good that he knew Darnell and where he lived. If Darnell did him this one favor, a courtesy, would the man leave him alone?

Was that it? Or was there something more? The way the man was pleading with him. There was something in his voice and manner, something that tugged at Darnell to find some means of helping him.

He can't come into the house, Darnell thought.

Darnell cast his eyes past the side of the house, toward the backyard. There was an old garden shed there. It was dilapidated and rotting. His parents had meant to have it demolished to make space for a new one, but then the virus had come, and everybody's plans had changed.

"Can you get up?" he asked.

"I don't know," the man said from under the bushes. "I'm weak."

"You can stay in the shed out back," Darnell said. "Can you make it there?"

"I'm welcome in your shed?"

Darnell paused. "What do you mean, *welcome*?"

"You have to come with me," the man said.

"I'm not touching you," Darnell said.

"Fair enough," the man said weakly. He started to stir, and Darnell backed up.

Darnell wrinkled his nose. There was that acrid smell again. The guy smelled bad. He needed more than a shed. He needed a shower and a decent place to stay.

He was so thin and frail, like a walking skeleton.

"Don't look at me," the man said, and that was enough for Darnell to allow himself to turn away.

"Follow me," Darnell told him. He made his way between the houses, moving slowly but not so slowly that the man would touch him again or get within his personal space bubble, until he reached the shed. Darnell stole a glance over his shoulder. The man was hobbling, hunched, sick-looking. He waved his hands at Darnell.

"This is the shed," Darnell said, pointing to it.

"And I'm welcome there?"

"Uh, sure," Darnell said. "You're leaving tonight?"

The man didn't say anything. He pushed the door farther open (it was already ajar), and it creaked loudly and squealed on its hinges. The doorway was so warped and angled that the bottom of the door scraped against the poured-concrete foundation and stuck there. Sunlight tried to punch into the shed, but there was always a deep darkness about the place that made Darnell never want to go in.

The stranger slipped inside, and Darnell turned away. He heard the scrape of the door as it closed, and when he turned around again, the shed door was firmly shut.

Darnell stood there, staring at it. He wondered if what had just happened was real. He wondered if he should tell his parents. He wondered why he was even thinking of *not* telling his parents. It went against everything his mind and body were telling him, just as they'd told him not to let this guy into his house.

He'd check the shed the next day.

In the morning Darnell opened the blinds of his window and saw the hummingbird feeder in the backyard. He couldn't remember it being there before. Maybe it had been there for days and he just hadn't noticed it.

But no. He spent so much time in and around the house that every little detail, every new crease and crack in the wall, every minute change, even a book put back on a certain shelf, stuck out to him.

"Did you put the hummingbird feeder out?" he asked his father.

"Don't think so," his father replied. He was busy at work on his laptop. He barely turned his head.

"Somebody put the bird feeder out there," Darnell said.

"Maybe we did it last week," his father suggested.

"I don't think we did," Darnell said. His memory was foggy—so many of the days tended to bleed together. But he didn't recall putting it out. No, he couldn't have.

His father kept working.

His mother was busy with Tyson, who was only three and needed a wrangler to keep him from destroying the house.

"Bird feeder?" she said.

"It's out in the backyard."

She shrugged as Tyson threw a handful of LEGO bricks across the floor. "It's possible," she said.

Still, it bothered Darnell that he couldn't remember anyone putting up the feeder. Then it occurred to him—the feeder had been in the shed. Where the sickly man had been.

"I'm going to check on it," Darnell said.

"Okay," she said.

The feeder was working, at any rate. Before Darnell had even gotten close, he spied the colorful blur of hummingbirds zipping through the air, stopping to hover at the feeder, often for just a few seconds, and then zipping off again. They were clearly interested in the red sugar solution, but thinking about it, who wasn't interested in sugar water? Darnell, always a big fan of energy drinks, couldn't blame the wee birds for drinking what he'd have happily gulped down himself.

He realized he was keeping his thoughts focused on the birds because it distracted him from the real reason he had come out.

Gathering his courage, Darnell approached the shed. The door was still closed.

"Hello?" he called out.

But there wasn't any answer.

Darnell looked at his hand. He wasn't wearing a glove. Had the man touched the doorknob? The virus could linger on surfaces...

He'd had some kind of illness, hadn't he? He was bloodied, and there was that acrid smell about him.

Why hadn't Darnell called the police? Or an ambulance?

Why hadn't he told his parents?

The man had been so convincing, Darnell told himself. *Just for the night.* But the door was shut, and Darnell needed to know that he was gone.

He gripped the knob, gave it a turn and pushed the door open so that the morning light spilled into the shed.

"CLOSE THE DOOR!" a voice screamed from inside.

Darnell jumped back.

He stood there, heart hammering in his chest. Through the opening, he saw a flicker of movement. A thin white figure moving toward the door and slamming it shut.

Darnell looked at his hand again.

Don't touch your face, he thought to himself. Go back to the house. Call for help.

"I know I said I'd leave," a muffled voice called from within. "I'm sorry, but I'm just not ready yet."

Darnell didn't move, though his mind told him to run. "Why are you still in our shed?"

"I need another day," the man said from inside.

"You said you'd be gone in the morning."

"I know what I said."

Darnell stood his ground. There was space between him and the door, and between the door and the man. He surveyed the shed. There was a window on the side, but already Darnell could see that the man had shoved a box in front of it to block the light—and the view inside. Clearly he did not want to be seen.

"You put out the feeder."

"Yes."

"Why?'"

"I thought I was doing you a favor."

Darnell narrowed his eyes. "Did we have the bird nectar in there?"

There was a moment's silence. "Of course you did," the man said.

Darnell remembered packing the feeder away in the fall. Would they have kept liquids in the shed even though they could freeze during the winter? He couldn't recall.

He heard something buzzing behind his ear and turned. A blur of motion caught his eye as another hummingbird went to the feeder, drank quickly and fluttered off.

"It's working," Darnell told him.

"Good," the man said.

And then, even though Darnell wasn't sure why, out came the words "I'm Darnell."

Another pause.

"My name is Mr. Sallow," the man inside the shed returned. And after a moment: "You saved my life. Thank you."

"What were you doing outside my house?"

"I got tired."

"You didn't look well. Are you sick? Can I call a doctor?"

"Don't call anybody," the man said, just like the day before, with a firmness that made Darnell uneasy.

"But you're sick—"

"It's nothing contagious," the man snapped back quickly and then said nothing further.

But Darnell looked at his naked hand and shivered. He needed hand sanitizer. Now. "I've got to go," he said. Then, to the closed door in front of him, he added, "You're just staying for the day, right?"

Another hummingbird buzzed past Darnell on its way to the feeder. There were a lot of them around.

"I'll be gone before you know it," said Mr. Sallow.

Darnell nodded, then quickly went back inside the house and washed his hands. You only needed to lather them with soap for thirty seconds, but Darnell kept washing until his hands were raw.

Darnell didn't tell his parents. Not yet. He was the one who'd helped Mr. Sallow. It was his fault Mr. Sallow was still in their shed. But Mr. Sallow was weak. He didn't have much strength. He needed help, but Darnell knew what his parents would say. To call the police.

The thoughts in his head wheeled around like the tires of his bike as he pedaled up and down the street, trying to figure out what to do.

It bothered him that he wasn't following his own instincts, that he kept delaying his decision.

But the farther away from his house he got, the easier it got to make a choice. Mr. Sallow had to go. Darnell had been kind. He'd more than gone out of his way to help, but enough was enough.

Darnell turned the bike around and sped toward home. He'd almost made it to his driveway.

Then he noticed it.

He clambered off his bike and stood there, numb.

Splotches of red dotted the driveway.

Something buzzed past one ear. Then the other. He looked up and saw them zipping through the trees, in and out of the foliage. Lots of hummingbirds, ruby-throated. With their fast movements, so quick that they were hard to catch or even count, Darnell saw only flashes of red.

But then he felt something on his face. Raindrops? There were few clouds overhead, and the sun was still blazing.

He raised a hand to his face.

Don't touch your face, he warned himself.

Felt something warm smear across his cheek.

Don't touch it!

Pulled his hand back and saw red.

It's blood*! It's blood!*

Then looked back to the red speckles on the driveway.

The hummingbirds are bleeding?

Then he heard whimpers from up ahead and saw the hummingbirds moving in toward a shape by the side door of the garage where the mailbox was.

Mr. Sallow?

Darnell broke into a run.

No, not Mr. Sallow.

The mail carrier was there, swatting at the hummingbirds. They were attacking him, zipping toward him, their beaks long and pointed.

"Get them off me!" he shouted.

Darnell stopped. Saw the blood pooling on the ground at the mail carrier's knees. Hummingbirds were flying there too, landing quickly, their small, snakelike tongues lapping up the blood.

Others poked at the mail carrier's face, his hands, his neck. More speckles of red, and the flutter of wings, and the loud buzzing as the birds darted about. Darnell stood in shock, not believing what he was seeing.

There was so much movement, such a frenzy of flailing arms and zipping birds. Yes, they were sticking their beaks into the mail carrier's flesh.

Impossible!

"Get them off me!" the mail carrier shouted again, and this time Darnell broke out of his daze.

He swatted at the birds, grabbing one and yanking it from the back of the mail carrier's hand. In one move he threw it as hard as he could. The bird careened fast toward the tarmac of the driveway, but before it could hit the ground, it beat its wings and took to the air again.

Shakily the mail carrier got to his knees. More spatters of red hit the pavement, and Darnell realized he'd come too close to the man.

Darnell backed away as the mail carrier got to his feet. The hummingbirds were still coming, but now Darnell was swatting at them.

Why weren't they attacking him? he wondered.

"Go!" Darnell said, urging the man on. "Run!"

Darnell watched the man flee. The hummingbirds followed him for a moment, but the postal worker, although weakened, managed to retreat down the block. The birds gave up their pursuit. Darnell was panting, the sweat pooling in the small of his back, soaking his shirt.

There was blood on his shirt. Was it his?

He looked at his hands, flecked with red.

Get inside.

He turned away and ran for the front door.

Wash your hands, tell your parents, call the police!

He'd gripped the handle, about to push the door in, when he heard the hummingbirds buzz past him.

Instinctive fear froze him to the spot as Darnell waited for the bladelike beaks of the birds to stab into him. Waiting for them to feast.

Another buzz. They were all zipping past him. To the backyard.

The feeder!

Darnell shook his head. Why had they attacked the mail carrier?

He took a step away from the house, moved carefully alongside it, rounded the corner, casting his eyes down so he could avoid seeing the small pool of blood by the mailbox—only the blood was nearly gone. The birds had lapped it all up.

But birds don't drink blood.

He saw them in the backyard, flitting in and out of view. He thought they might be moving around the feeder, but he saw when he got there that it wasn't where they were going at all.

The hummingbirds were flitting around the shed, bumping against the one window like they were trying to get inside.

He watched the birds, not understanding.

Then the door creaked open and the hummingbirds disappeared inside, one after the other. Darnell's mouth dropped open.

"Mr. Sallow!"

They were there to feed on him too! Darnell lunged forward, pushed the door open with his weight and tumbled into the shed with such force that he toppled to the dirty cement floor.

He looked up. Sunlight filtered into the dingy space, illuminating swirls of dust motes, and there in the corner, cowering under the old burlap sack Darnell's parents had left there, was Mr. Sallow, the birds buzzing around him.

"Mr. Sallow, you're going to be okay."

Darnell got to his feet. Took a few steps into the shed. Mr. Sallow was sitting with his face turned away from the open doorway, his back to Darnell. Why wasn't he trying to get out of there, away from the birds?

Was he—?

Darnell took another step forward and saw.

The birds were on him, but they weren't pecking or stabbing. They were waiting.

Something else.

A sound.

Like sucking. Swallowing. Gulping.

"Mr. Sallow?"

Darnell took another step forward, his shadow blotting out the sunlight from the open doorway, and finally the man turned.

Darnell had seen Mr. Sallow before, but thinking about it now, had he *really* looked at the man's face?

Mr. Sallow's eyes were wide, set so deep in their sockets that it looked like someone had pushed them to the back of his skull. His skin was bone white and pulled so tight against his face that the bones jutted out.

The pallor made the dripping red blood stand out even more. It was all around his mouth, dribbling down his chin.

Mr. Sallow held a bird in his hand. What was he doing? Was he…eating it?

No, not eating.

Darnell saw the bird. Saw the trickle of red dripping out of its beak and into Mr. Sallow's open mouth. The man's tongue lapping up the blood.

Mr. Sallow's eyes flared in surprise, then recognition. He pulled the bird away, and it buzzed over to a dusty shelf in the corner of the shed. "Get out."

"Mr. Sallow—"

He stood. "Get out!"

Darnell backed away, tumbling into another shelf. The sunlight pierced the spot where Mr. Sallow was standing, and he recoiled, scowling at the light. He hissed, pointing a bony finger at Darnell. "GET OUT!"

Darnell got out, slamming the door behind him.

For a while Darnell just sat in his room. If he wanted to, he could stand by the window, and if he pressed his face right up to the edge, he could see the far corner of the shed. He was unable to see the door to tell if it was open or shut. He'd hoped Mr. Sallow had finally left.

But he hadn't. He was in the shed. He'd had blood on his mouth.

The blood from the birds.

Or, rather, the blood from that postal carrier.

He closed his blinds and rocked back and forth on his bed. The images of Mr. Sallow wouldn't leave his mind, no matter how hard he tried to block them out. He'd put on music, flipped through a book. Nothing worked.

Later he came downstairs to tell his parents, but they were busy with Tyson, playing games that toddlers like to play.

"Dad," Darnell began.

His father, usually too busy with work or Tyson to give Darnell the time of day, looked up. "Do you want to play? Your brother is amazing at knocking blocks down."

Darnell shook his head.

"You okay, Darnell?"

"The feeder," Darnell said.

"Yeah, I saw that," his father replied. "Thanks for setting it up. Good idea. Lots of hummingbirds about."

"More than we're used to seeing," his mother chimed in.

"Birds!" exclaimed Tyson, and knocked down the tower of blocks his father had just set up.

Darnell opened his mouth to tell them, but stopped. Why couldn't he say it? Darnell hadn't called the police, told his parents or done any of the things his mind had screamed at him to do. Like Mr. Sallow *wasn't allowing* him to call.

But Mr. Sallow wasn't safe.

Mr. Sallow needed to stay in the shed, Darnell thought to himself. He wasn't safe out of it.

Darnell never had thoughts like these.

Darnell's dad had already gone back to playing with Tyson.

Were his own parents safe? What if he told his dad, and his dad went to the shed, and Mr. Sallow was in the shed? Mr. Sallow got the birds to attack that mail carrier. Was it better to just wait? If he just waited, would Mr. Sallow leave?

Darnell did not go back outside.

Instead he sat by the window, looking out into the yard.

He watched for the birds. Every once in a while, a hummingbird would swoop down to the feeder and drink.

What if he went out to the feeder and took it down? Would that help? Was it safe?

He kept staring out the window, thinking. By the time he'd gathered his thoughts, the sun was already going down, and it was time for dinner.

The tapping woke Darnell up. It sounded like a branch at his window, pushed by the wind. *Tap. Tap. Tap.*

There was only one small problem.

There were no tree branches outside Darnell's window.

Slowly he sat up in his bed.

Tap. Tap. Tap.

Another thought. What if it was one of those hummingbirds? Or more than one?

Darnell's feet touched the carpet. He stood up. He paced to the window. The blinds were closed, but if he opened them just a crack, he could look out between the slats.

Tap. Tap. Tap.

He pushed the blinds apart, just a sliver.

He peeked out.

Staring back at him through the gap was a pair of eyes.

Darnell jumped back, heart pounding.

He ran back to his bed and pulled up the covers. *Make it stop!*

"Darnelllllllll," a voice called from the other side of the window.

Tap. Tap. Tap.

Darnell lay under the covers, shivering.

"Come on, Darnell. I just want to talk."

It was impossible. His room was on the second floor. Nobody could get up that high. Unless...

Was there a ladder in the shed? Had Mr. Sallow found it?

"It's not like you invited me inside."

Mr. Sallow's words hung in the air. Darnell thought about this.

The man drank blood. He hated the sun. He had to be invited inside.

Slowly Darnell pulled back the covers. He approached the window. He didn't need to open the blinds farther to know that Mr. Sallow hadn't taken a ladder, that he was floating of his own accord, because that's what his kind did.

"I know what you are," Darnell said, breaking the silence.

"Finally figured it out, eh? Go on, say it."

Darnell took a deep breath and pulled the cord so that the blinds fully opened.

"*Vampire,*" Darnell said, trying to be brave, trying to stare at the monster on the other side of the glass.

Mr. Sallow tapped against the glass, and Darnell could see his fingernails—longer now, pointed and gnarled.

"Why are you here? Why me?"

"You let me into your shed," he said. "You *welcomed* me in, Darnell."

"That's not what I meant. Why don't you go back to your house?"

"Nobody comes there," he rasped, his voice sounding hungry, "and I need to feed."

Mr. Sallow was not well. He was weak. The sunlight was too much for him. He couldn't roam around by day, and nobody was out at night. The virus had kept people off the streets.

"You think this has been easy for me?" Mr. Sallow said. "With the virus, everybody stays inside, so there's nowhere to feed. And if nobody goes out, then I have to come *in*. But nobody welcomes anyone into their homes anymore. Well, except you."

Darnell's heart caught in his throat. "You're *not* welcome in my house."

"Not the house, but the shed."

Darnell almost choked. It was true. He'd let Mr. Sallow in there. How could he have been so foolish? "I'll tell my father. We'll call the police."

"Will you? You didn't before."

Darnell thought about this. "But I wanted to?" It was more like a question, the way it came out. Why *hadn't* he told his parents? Then he realized. "You're getting into my thoughts," Darnell said.

A smile spread across Mr. Sallow's face, and this time two sharp fangs poked out from under his lips.

"Don't worry, Darnell. You saved my life. I owe you."

There were things Darnell needed to know, though. "What did you do to the hummingbirds?"

"I needed to feed. Needed to find something to bring me my food."

Darnell shook his head. "But they eat sugar water. We didn't leave the sugar water in the shed."

"No, you didn't."

"Then what—?" Darnell stopped himself. What was red? What was liquid? What had the birds been drinking? "Blood?" Deep down he supposed he'd known. But he retched a bit just thinking of it.

"Blood is life," Mr. Sallow intoned.

"They almost *killed* the mail carrier."

"Better him than you, right? That's what I wanted to talk to you about, Darnell. I see your thoughts. I see how you keep meaning to tell your parents, to call the police."

"You can't kill people—"

"I need to feed. And if you are going to be a burden, consider our deal at an end."

"What deal?"

"The one where you get to live," Mr. Sallow said, and with that he drifted away from the blinds, disappearing into the cloak of night.

When Darnell woke again, it wasn't to the sound of tapping on his window, which was a relief. Instead he heard the gleeful squeals of Tyson playing. It took him a second to realize that they were coming from outside.

Darnell bolted out of bed and raced to his window. He yanked on the cord, and the blinds flew up.

"Tyson!"

He was there, in the backyard, playing with their mom and dad. Playing right by the bird feeder. There was still red fluid in it. There were still hummingbirds flitting to and fro. Darnell's blood froze.

He flashed a glance at his clock. How long had he slept in?

Didn't matter. He threw on his clothes and ran down the stairs, through the kitchen and out the sliding door to the backyard.

"You've got to come back inside!" he shouted at them, waving his hands. "It's not safe!"

"Not safe?" his father said.

"It's a lovely day," said his mother.

"Play, Darnell! Play!" said Tyson.

Darnell stopped looking at them. Looked past them, at the feeder, then beyond, to the shed. The door was closed.

"He's here," Darnell managed to say, letting the warnings that had been bouncing around his head for the past two days finally come out. "He's in the shed, and he's dangerous."

"Who's dangerous?" asked his mother.

"Mr. Sallow," Darnell said, the words barely escaping his lips. Because now he could see something at the corner of Tyson's mouth.

A line.

A red line dripping from the corner of his mouth.

"Tyson?"

Darnell heard the low-frequency buzz of a passing hummingbird and recoiled in horror. One zipped past him, then another. The first came to land on the feeder. The second loop-de-looped around Tyson, coming to land on his shoulder.

Tyson squealed with delight.

The bird remained still, even as Tyson grabbed hold of it with his little hand.

"Tyson, no!"

Even as Tyson brought it up to his mouth.

Darnell watched. Unable to move.

Even as the hummingbird's beak went right up to Tyson's lips, and the blood trickled from the bird's mouth to his own.

"Mom," Darnell said. "Didn't you see—?"

Darnell's mother smiled. And when she did, Darnell saw the red stains on her teeth, on her tongue.

"No, Mom," Darnell said weakly. "Not you too."

"It's okay," Darnell's father said, red liquid dribbling down his chin. "It's okay." He stood up and walked over to Darnell, putting a hand on his shoulder. Darnell could smell his father's sour breath, like he hadn't brushed his teeth in weeks. "Mr. Sallow promised us eternal life. All we have to do is drink."

"Yummy, Darnell!" Tyson squealed. "You try too!"

Darnell shook his head, pressing his lips shut.

"You must," his father said. "We're all going to drink. And then we're just going to wait until it gets a little bit darker."

Darnell looked past his father to the shed, where the door opened. Just a crack. Just a sliver. And even then Darnell could see the outline of the thing inside.

"Just until it's safe for Mr. Sallow to come out of that cramped old shed," his father continued, "and into the house. After all, he's our guest. And he's most, *most* welcome."

part five

As soon as she saw the announcement, Tanya knew what to do.

After all this time, a year later, Joel Southland was coming back to her school. For this visit, Tanya made sure to sit much closer to the action.

She'd had a lot more time to think about how she might reencounter Southland. In fact, she was the one who'd suggested to Ms. Monroe that the school invite him back. He was certainly a popular author.

Tanya kept a low profile as the rest of the students were ushered into the library for the presentation. She'd asked Ms. Monroe to introduce her to Southland. She wondered if he would remember her. If he still knew that this was her school.

These thoughts bubbled in her brain until the moment came, and Southland walked through the doors into the library.

Ms. Monroe pulled Tanya over to him. "Mr. Southland, I'd like you to meet one of our star young authors. This is—"

But Southland silenced Ms. Monroe with a wave of his hand before she could get another word in. "Oh, we've met," he said with a wink.

Tanya felt her muscles tighten.

Southland extended a welcoming hand for Tanya to shake. "It's Tanya, isn't it?"

Tanya nodded. She stared at his hand with the same sort of caution she might reserve for a live electrical wire or a cobra being handed to her. But she had to do what she had to do, so she shook his hand. Or rather she let Joel Southland shake her hand. His grip was tight and firm and full of malice.

She dared herself to meet his steely gaze.

She didn't say anything about their other run-ins. And Southland did not mention the library meeting, or nearly running her over with his car, or the ink.

He leaned in a bit closer. "I think one day you are going to make a great author," he said with a barely discernable grimace.

"That's what I like to say," Ms. Monroe chirped, completely unaware of the tension between the two.

"I do have some stories kicking around in my head," Tanya admitted.

But Southland didn't say anything further.

Tanya was trying to figure out if Southland knew she had recognized him not just from his author visits but from the night when he'd thrown the ink at her, when she'd caught him at Cindy's. The ink took your dreams and made you forget them, but was it supposed to erase memories of other times as well— and of the ink itself?

"I do have one question for you," Tanya said at last. "Where *do* you get your ideas?""

She gave Southland a knowing glance, looking right into his eyes. She didn't expect the truth. Not in front of the rest of the classes assembled in the library. And as she anticipated, he gave the exact same answer he'd given before. Like he said it at every school he visited. "I do get lots of ideas from these school visits. From talking to you about all the things you fear. I like to work your fears into my stories. It's what makes them more real."

"You really do work our fears into your stories," Tanya said with a sly smile. "Keep up the good work."

Joel Southland stepped into the hotel room and closed the door behind him. Seeing all these kids exhausted him, but it paid for such nice, fancy rooms.

The first thing he did was take his jacket off and put it on the chair by the desk. Then he placed his satchel down on the chair beside him and pulled out his laptop computer and the envelope with the money the school had given him. And then he saw it.

A handwritten note.

He could tell it was written by a kid, and immediately he knew who had penned it.

That girl *knew*. She had to.

Why had they crossed paths so many times?

She kept popping up, and not just like your average super-fan. She'd seen him in the car, with the ink. Had she been following him?

But it couldn't be! He'd thrown the ink at her, and the ink extracted her dreams and memories. It was meant to protect him. It had told him as much. He hadn't harvested that latest story of hers yet, although the first nightmare the ink extracted from her was deliciously terrifying.

The ink had done so much for him over these past years. Did it matter that a few children lost their dreams and a few select memories? It was a small price to pay for his own success, and besides, the ink needed to feed.

He could tell the ink was growing restless. It was looking for more potent dreams to feast upon.

Maybe it would be a good idea to go back and visit that kid again.

She was onto him, but he could solve that. He'd done it before, and he would do it again. There were other kids who'd figured out the secret—or almost had. He'd found ways to make them forget about him. But maybe...

Southland paced around the room, shaking his head. Maybe he could find ways to make people forget about those kids.

Yes, he realized. He could do that. The ink would take care of it all.

Then he could stop worrying about this snooping girl, get back to the dirty business of stories and books. There were so many other kids, so many other schools. They all bled together into a meaningless group of fans. It didn't matter as long as they kept buying his books, and as long as the schools kept paying him to come and give his presentation.

He picked up the note and began to read.

I know you remember me, Mr. Southland. But I thought this would be a better way to communicate. It wouldn't do to have to explain ourselves in front of the school. And I have a lot to explain, after all this time.

You see, I found out the secret to your stories.

I wasn't sure at first. I remember you gave me a bookmark, and then I had a scary dream. At first I thought that part of my dream was about the ink on the bookmark coming alive. Of course, that part wasn't my dream. I didn't remember my dream, not for a good long while. Not until it came out several months later in one of your stories.

You don't actually write the world's scariest stories. You steal them from our dreams, and you put them into your books. The ink on those bookmarks you hand out does the work for you. It's alive. It talks to you.

Well, guess what? The ink talks to me too.

For example, it came up with the idea of writing you a note. I didn't want to. I was afraid of what might happen, but the ink told me what would happen if I didn't. But then, you know all about listening to the ink, don't you?

That's why you keep it with you at all times. Even just a little bit, like in the pen in your jacket. You write autographs when the ink tells you to. But the ink has been writing to me lately.

Southland put the paper down. He went to his jacket and reached inside for the pocket. His eyes went wide as he realized the pen was missing.

For a long while Southland went through his belongings—all the things he'd taken with him to the school. His jacket, his bag. He turned out the pockets, dumped the contents of the satchel onto the floor, and began sifting through papers and piles of thumb drives and other junk, but it still wasn't there. The pen! That girl had the pen! And she knew...

His heart racing, Southland went back to the letter and continued to read.

You've been giving the same presentation each time, year after year, right? You show us pictures and get us to write stories. But you don't read them. They're not what you're really after.

It's our dreams, isn't it?

You use the ink to take them out of us.

The ink has spoken to me now. It thinks you are getting too lazy. Success has gone to your head. It's looking for new dreams to feed on. It thinks yours would do nicely.

By now I'm sure you'll have recognized the ink I wrote this with. It's from that pen of yours. I'm sure you've been reading long enough for the ink to work. I guess you'll find out soon enough.

From Tanya.
P.S. Stay scared!

Southland put the paper down. His hands were shaking. His skin had gone pale, and already beads of sweat were pushing through his pores and running down in little rivers.

The girl had used *so much ink!*

He only used enough to sign his name. That's all he'd *ever* used. Well, except for when he'd thrown it at Tanya. The ink was potent, like cobra venom.

She must not have realized its potency. Or maybe she did.

The paper on the floor began to flutter. Southland shook his head, backing away from it. He dared not touch it. He could see the letters of the note beginning to bleed together, until a large black puddle oozed off the page and moved across the floor toward him.

He turned to run, but the ink was too fast. It slid under his feet, tripping him up. Southland crashed to the floor, falling hard on his chin.

He tasted blood in his mouth, flipped over, and there it was, coiled and snakelike and stretching his way. The ink was fast, the ink was cold, and the ink was on his arms, racing up toward his face, his eyes, his—

Outside the hotel-room door, Tanya blinked once. Twice.

She watched as a ribbon of black liquid oozed out from under the door and into her shoe. Her foot felt wet and cold and—

And—

Tanya closed her eyes and smiled. Out of the blue, she had an idea. A great and terrible idea. Maybe it was hers, and maybe it wasn't. No matter. She turned around and walked down the hallway to the elevator.

She held the idea in her head and let it brew. All she needed was a pen and a sheet of paper. What a great story it would make!

STAY SCARED!

Joel Southland

JEFF SZPIRGLAS is the author of several works for young people, including the horror collections *Tales from Beyond the Brain* and *Tales from the Fringes of Fear*. He is also the co-author, with Danielle Saint-Onge, of a number of Orca Echoes titles, including *Shark Bait!*, *X Marks the Spot!* and *Messy Miranda*. Jeff has worked at CTV and was an editor at *Chirp*, *Chickadee* and *Owl* magazines. In his spare time, he teaches grade school. Jeff lives with his family in Kitchener, Ontario.

STEVEN P. HUGHES is an award-winning Canadian illustrator whose clients include the *Globe and Mail*, *Reader's Digest* and *Scientific American*. He graduated from Sheridan College with a BAA in illustration. He lives in Bolton, Ontario.